PATRICK HENRY'S SECRET IN THE CELLAR

a story of his insane wife Sarah Shelton

outskirts
press

ACKNOWLEDGMENTS

I want to thank again three Shelton descendants for their knowledge and love of the Shelton family. These three Shelton descendants started my path to researching deeper into the story of Sarah Shelton Henry. Sarah Shelton Henry was a woman that history chose not to talk about, whether it was because of lack of information about Sarah Henry or possibly fear it would be an embarrassment for the Henry family. Patrick Henry was working on making a change for the better for the colony. Mr. Henry had spent many years struggling to reach a point in his life where he felt like he could make a change for the better. These were times in American history when families felt like there could not be an embarrassing situation in the family. The Patrick Henry family had to live day in and day out with a dark secret!

These three Shelton descendants are from the Norfolk England Shelton line. Their lineage as well as mine can be traced back to James Shelton 1st (ca. 1580-1668). This James Shelton arrived at Jamestown Virginia (ca. 1610) along with a relative, Thomas West, Lord De La Warr.

These three Shelton descendants are: Judge Dale Shelton, Arkansas County, Arkansas; Downing Abbott Bolls Sr., Taylor County, Texas; and Dr. William A. Shelton, Mecklenburg

County, Virginia.

The characters in this book are fictitious. They are based on research done on the Patrick Henry family and extended families. This fictional book is based on situations that may have happened to the Patrick Henry family during the colonial period in American history. The names have been changed and in no way show any disrespect to any family name or any of their descendants. The characters of Abigail Lewis and Ruben Lewis are based on Sarah Shelton and Patrick Henry of Hanover County, Virginia. I write this book to show respect to a woman that history has never recognized as much more than the first wife of Patrick Henry.

TABLE OF CONTENTS

INTRODUCTION

Sarah Shelton Henry was the daughter of John Shelton and Eleanor Parks of Hanover County, Virginia. They were a very well respected family. Sarah Shelton Henry's ancestors can be traced back to the reign of King Henry VIII and Queen Anne Boleyn of England.

Sarah Shelton Henry's maternal grandfather was William Parks, the first newspaper editor of Virginia

I write this book hoping to show some of the feelings, both mentally and physically, that Sarah Shelton Henry may have experienced after the birth of her last child—feelings that women today are still experiencing. These feelings, if not properly treated, can and have led to very unhappy, unstable, and possibly suicidal women. These are feelings that these women do not understand; are feelings and actions that their families do not understand. These are feelings that these women have never experienced before. They do not know how to handle these feelings that sometimes come to these women without warning.

These feelings, mentally and physically, have always been around. Women have experienced these feelings throughout the history of mankind. They did not know how to explain why some women would change into someone who could be dangerous to herself and to her family as well. Only in recent years has the medical world put a name to it; it's called postpartum psychosis.

There seems to be different levels of the psychosis. Some women suffer more than others.

Through my research I have found that Sarah Shelton Henry must have suffered a number of years with what Preservation Virginia seems to think was postpartum psychosis.

Preservation Virginia says Patrick Henry's private doctor was Dr. Thomas Hinde. Dr Hinde was born in England. He practiced medicine in Virginia and later moved to Kentucky.

Years after the death of Dr. Thomas Hinde his son was looking through some of his father's papers. In these papers were notes that Dr. Hinde had made on some of his visits to the Henry's plantation, Scotchtown. These notes would have probably been written between 1771 and 1775.

One of the notes made reference to a visit Dr. Hinde had made to Scotchtown. It said that not only did the doctor find Sarah Shelton Henry confined to the cellar of their home but he also found Sarah Henry wearing a "Quaker Dress." That would probably be what we think of today as a medical straitjacket. Obviously this is something that Mr. Henry made Sarah Henry wear, possibly so she could not hurt herself or others.

Preservation Virginia also makes reference to a possible trapdoor that was in the back part of the house that would take you to the cellar. I do not know if Dr. Hinde made any reference to a trapdoor in his notes. There were other entrances to the cellar as well.

Research shows that Patrick Henry's mother wrote a letter to her daughter. She wrote, "We feel Sarah is losing her mind after the birth of little Neddy."

Preservation Virginia also says the Henry's oldest daughter, Martha, was asked to come back to Scotchtown shortly after her marriage to live and to help care for her mother. Martha Henry and her husband, John Fontaine, did go back to Scotchtown to live. Martha Henry Fontaine's first child, Patrick Henry Fontaine, was born at Scotchtown. Martha Henry Fontaine was politically a great help to her father, Patrick Henry, after the death of Sarah Henry and their move from Scotchtown.

The cellar floor where Sarah Shelton Henry is said to have lived for three or four years is said to have been a dirt floor at the time of Sarah Henry's confinement in the cellar.

Preservation Virginia also refers to a female slave that Mr. Henry had living in the cellar with his wife. This slave was thought to have lived in the cellar with Sarah Henry until her death. Most research shows that Sarah Shelton Henry died in that cellar in early spring of 1775.

Sarah Shelton Henry did not choose to live or die in that cellar. Patrick Henry was left with the heart-wrenching decision as to what to do with his sick wife. It was a sickness or illness that no one knew anything about. Nothing! This was a woman that could have possibly changed mentally and physically into someone they did not even recognize.

Mr. Henry's private doctor did suggest the new hospital in Williamsburg. But Patrick Henry did not want his loving wife to live the rest of her life in a possibly filthy and dangerous room with nothing but straw for bedding and a chamber pot for waste. And Sarah Henry would have certainly been chained to a wall where she would have been very limited in her movements.

Patrick Henry could not find it in his heart to do that to the sweet girl that he had married years before, even if his wife may have changed mentally and physically into someone that maybe he did not even recognize.

If Sarah Shelton Henry did suffer from what is now thought to be postpartum psychosis then Sarah Henry very likely did have outbursts of rage, anger, and confusion and she possibly just had a sense of loss.

Sarah Shelton Henry is believed to be buried in an unmarked grave at the Henry's plantation, Scotchtown.

I
THE DOOR

Well look at that: Lizzy has forgotten to bolt my door. That's not like her to forget. If I had not gotten up to use the chamber pot I would have never noticed.

My door is always bolted. I want to leave and go for a walk—it's been so long since I did that. But I don't want Lizzy to hear me. I know if I leave I will have to be back before dawn; I don't want them to know I've been gone.

If I get caught they will always make sure my door is bolted. If Ruben found out I had left my room he would blame Lizzy. Lizzy has taken care of me for a long time it seems. Lizzy is good to me. She brushes my hair twice a day. When I get sad I sit on the ground in front of her with my head in her lap. She sings softly to me and tells me when I get better I can go upstairs and won't have to stay in the cellar anymore.

I don't know if I believe her or not. They always tell me things, but they don't come true.

The ground feels warm beneath my bare feet as I softly walk closer to my fireplace. If I put my shoes on Lizzy will surely hear me. But we've had a lot of rain, so if I don't wear shoes I'll catch a death of cold for sure. And it is cold out there!

I never get to leave the cellar. I miss my children! They used to do things to make me sad and make me scream. I remember one day when Sarah was wearing her rose-colored dress. She kept turning around and around. That would upset me so. She would just stand in place and turn around and around looking at me the whole time.

I asked her to stop but she just looked at me and kept right on dancing around the room while staring at me. Seems like Sarah was about seven then. All my children would upset me! That day when Sarah would not stop dancing I made her sit in a chair and I tied her ankles together with the sash from her dress. I thought, this will stop you!

Sarah started crying and you could hear her all throughout the house and probably all the way to the kitchen. Miss Sally come running in, thinking Sarah got hurt. I told Miss Sally that Sarah was not hurt! Miss Sally said,"Now Miss Abigail,you can't be doing stuff like this. You know this ain't right."

Then walked in Ruben, fussing like an old boar hog. When he saw Sarah crying he turned and looked at me and started screaming my name. I was standing in the middle of the floor screaming and crying, not understanding what was happening. I just wanted the child to be quiet! That's all I wanted!

Ruben was standing there with a dumb look on his face, with tears running down his cheeks, and he was still screaming at me. I could not stop crying and screaming. None of them understand how I feel!

Ruben had quickly pulled a small knife from his pocket and cut the sash from Sarah's ankles. While still screaming at me he threw the sash in my face and said, "Abby, what I'm I going to do with you!" Ruben has never understood how I feel. He does not want to understand. He won't talk to me! He never wants to listen to what I have to say.

Ruben wants Judith Anne and her family to move here since he's gone so much to either Richmond or Williamsburg. But Judith Anne said she told her father she could not bring her family here to live. I think Ruben was upset with her, but never would tell her so.

Ruben is gone all the time now. I don't know what he does on all those trips. Sometimes I hear him ride off before the crack of dawn. It's a lonely sound, hearing the last faint sounds of Ruben's horse as he makes his way down our winding road and onto the main road to Richmond.

Ruben will usually stay at a local inn. He has stayed at times at my parents' inn over in Hanover. I remember one winter he was there for two days. The inn is not that far from Cedar Grove, but the snow and ice were so deep that Ruben feared his horse might damage one of his legs.

If the truth be known, I think Ruben still likes staying at my parents tavern and inn. There's always someone there that Ruben enjoys talking to. The inn is on the main road so they usually have a lot of guests, and Miss Sissy is a good cook. Father says all his guests tell him how much they like the food there. I don't really know where Miss Sissy came from. She's always been there, as far as I know. Maybe she came from one of the Carter family's plantations. Miss Sissy never talked much, as far as I can remember.

I sure would like to get out of the cellar for a while. I'm so afraid I will get caught! And if I do Ruben will be so upset. He blames everything on me and Lizzy—things we do not even know about. If I try to talk to him he just turns around and walks out. He really does not come to the cellar that much, and I don't understand why he had to put that large bolt on my door. It's only me and Lizzy down here, and just the other day I could hear Benson doing something to the door.

Lizzy tells me everybody wants me to get better, but I don't believe her. If they all wanted me to get better they would let me leave the cellar and live upstairs with my family again.

II
UNCLE PETE AND MISS SALLY

Before they put me in the cellar I could go on some walks with Uncle Pete and Lizzy. I guess Uncle Pete was some kin to Lizzy. We all just called him Uncle Pete.

Ruben bought Uncle Pete from old Jake Carter's plantation, Sugar Ridge, not long after Ruben and I got married. Lizzy lived at Sugar Ridge before coming here to Cedar Grove too.

Miss Sally came from Sweet Pine. I don't think Sweet Pine was a nice place! One day before I got sick Miss Sally was telling me some stories about when she was a young girl. She said when she first got to Sweet Pine old Master Campbell was nice to his slaves, but after Miss Elizabeth died giving birth to her last child old Master Campbell just changed. He changed into somebody they didn't even know. He was mean to everybody, even his children. Old Master Campbell would beat the men for no reason.

Miss Sally said one day her older sister Lucy had told her she was with child. She said that old Master Campbell would go to Lucy's slave cabin even though he knew she was with child. She said he would pay that no mind. She remembered one night when old Master Campbell finished and left Lucy's cabin. Said that was a terrible, terrible night. Sally said she still cries when she thinks about it.

Sally said Lucy started bleeding and bled all night. Sally was young but she did remember running to the creek to get a bucket of water to wash Lucy up with. The next day one of the other slaves had to do her work and Lucy's too, because Lucy was no good that next day. She was so weak from losing so much blood.

Miss Sally sure did love Lucy. She said the last time Lucy was with child they found her floating in the creek. I don't guess she could take anymore hurting. I told Miss Sally I did not want to hear anymore of those sad stories. Sad stories always make me cry because I know how it feels to be hurt and sad.

Miss Sally told me she sure did not want me to cry. Sally said she was only telling me a story about somebody she loved very much. She told me she misses Lucy everyday.

I cried a lot before Ruben put me in the cellar to live. Ruben has never understood my feelings, and to make things worse he doesn't even want to listen to me. I had begged him to just let me go for some short walks, but he won't hear of it. And I beg and beg for him to sit down with me so we can talk like we used to.

At least the boys here on the plantation treat me and Lizzy good. They always keep us a good fire going with plenty of good wood down here. It's always damp and I can never get quite warm enough. Lizzy feels the same way too, but she just doesn't say it as much as I do. I guess she is scared of Ruben. I don't know, but he likes Lizzy and thinks a lot of her.

Miss Sally takes care of all my children now. I can hear them running through the house sometimes and can hear Sally telling them to be quiet and settle down some. She's always kind to them and they seem to love her a lot. I know I love her and always have. The eating room is right above my room so I can hear everyone when they are in there, especially Sarah and Edmund.

Miss Sally was part of my marriage dowry when I married Ruben. I guess my father bought Sally from old Mr. Campbell here in Hanover. Sally was one of our house slaves. She would help my mother, my sisters, and I. When I used to feel better I could walk over to the slave cabins and have Chassy mend some of my clothes.

Uncle Pete would usually be somewhere around and so many times would be scolding some of the young boys for something they either did or did not do. Uncle Pete seemed to think that most masters of plantations were somewhat good. He always would say that if they were not good it was cause the devil was in their hearts and souls. He thought all they really needed was a good soul cleansing.

When we would go walking Uncle Pete would always tell me," Miss Abilgail,you just be good and you can go back up-stairs to live someday." Uncle Pete was good to me. He would bring me wildflowers when they were in bloom. I would have

Lizzy get some water in a cup for my flowers. I would set them in the window and let the sunlight shine through them. When the sun would shine just right, all the colors from the flowers would be like little petals dancing in the air

I can look out my windows and see my children playing and everyone here at the plantation moving around. My windows are locked. Ruben made sure the windows were locked the day he put Lizzy and I down here. I am trapped in this cellar.

The door stays bolted and the windows are locked. There's no way out of here unless Ruben decides he wants me to live back upstairs again, and I don't believe that will ever happen! What few times I see Ruben I always beg him to let me get out of the cellar. He never listens to what I need. He just nods his head and goes back upstairs.

I sure do miss Uncle Pete. It seems he died so long ago, but Lizzy tells me it's only been about a year now. I did get to go to his burying, but Ruben made sure that Old Joe and Lizzy were right there with me. Uncle Pete is buried in our slave cemetery just a little south of the main house. Ruben has some of the younger boys keep the cemetery cleaned up.

They keep it nice. Uncle Pete would be proud of them. He always wanted young folks to do good. He used to say if the young folks worked hard when they were young, they would turn out to be good folks. He also said lazy folks don't amount to nothing. I miss him! It's still makes me cry when I think of him and what a good person he was. He was a good man and I think he was happy here at Cedar Grove. He always seemed to be.

III
OLD MR. STEARS

Ruben made our overseer John Stears leave Cedar Grove.
Ruben said he did not want any kind of beatings at all at his
plantation. Lizzy told me Mr. Stears was talking back to Ruben,
telling him some of those young boys just wouldn't do what
they were supposed to do.

Lizzy said Ruben got real mad and was real red in the face
and looked like he wanted to hit the old man. Lizzy said the
old man kept talking back to Ruben even after Ruben had told
him to shut up.

She said Ruben could hardly get a word in, and I know that
made him so upset because that man does like to talk!

Chassy walked up when Lizzy and I were talking. She told
us that Mr. Ruben was very upset with old Mr. Stears. Ruben
had told him he better not ever hear of anybody being beaten
again.

Only a few days later Chassy came back to the cellar and
was telling me and Lizzy that Ruben had walked right up on
the old man and he was beating another young boy.

I think it was Chloe's boy . . . I can't remember. But Chassy
had said Chloe had to stay up all night with the boy cause he

was in so much pain. They say the scars will never go away because they are so deep.

They say Ruben grabbed the whip right out of the old man's hand and told him to leave Cedar Grove right then.

Ruben is good to everybody I guess, but he is not good to me anymore cause he's the one that put me here in the cellar. I don't think Ruben loves me anymore. What if Ruben had to live down here! I don't think he would like that at all. Ruben likes to talk to people too much, so I know he would hate it down here, just like I do.

Before I had to come to the cellar I heard Ruben's mother talking to Lizzy about me. I heard her tell Lizzy she thought I was losing my mind, but that old bag is the one who is crazy! Then the old bag had something to say about my little Edmund. Edmund is my little boy. He's about three now, I guess. I'm not sure because I do lose track of time.

I remember her trying to tell Ruben what to do, and I really think he listens to her a lot. So much of what she would say I would disagree with, cause she don't know half the time what she's talking about. When I would try to say something to Ruben about her he would get so upset with me. I think she is the reason that Ruben put me down here in the cellar. I really think it's her fault! I think she had Ruben put me down here so no one could see and really know what's going on here at Cedar Grove.

I remember one afternoon when Ruben was reading in the library. The old woman walked right in on him, never knocking or anything. I couldn't hear everything, but most of what I

OLD MR. STEARS

did hear did not make sense to me. I did hear my name once or twice, so I know they were talking about me.

I always hated it when Ruben's mother would say "now Abigail do you think you should do that " She never approved of anything that I did. I know she's the reason I'm down in the cellar right now

Lizzy tells me that's not true But I don't believe her! That's another lie that's been told, just like all the other lies they tell me.

The old bag was also telling Ruben about how people in Virginia like to talk. She told Ruben he better be careful and not let this kind of thing get out. I never really knew what she was talking about.

So much of what people said didn't make any sense to me at all. I wish John Stears had of taken a whip to her backside. I think the old man had it in him.

11

IV
EDMUND'S CELEBRATION

Edmund was my last child born. He was the smallest of all my children, and he was the one that seemed to give me the most trouble. He cried all the time! Then I would get so upset I would start crying. I felt as if my head would explode.

No one wanted to listen to how I felt and they still don't. Miss Sally would come from wherever she was and take little Edmund from me. I did not like that! Someone taking my baby from me, that ain't right!

Even though I have six children none of them come down to the cellar to see me much. I guess they don't care anymore about me. What's wrong with all these people! I've always been nice to them. They don't seem to want to be around me anymore.

My Catherine Louise used to come down to the cellar often. We would read some and sometimes she would bring something to paint down here. But now she has become Miss Prissy! She doesn't come much anymore. I asked her why she doesn't and she just gave me some kind of lame excuse. They've all got excuses!

My son Madison comes down more often than any of the

rest. I believe it was the first fall after Ruben put Lizzy and I down here that we had a big celebration for my little Edmund.

We had a large dinner and more apple pies than we could eat. It had been a good year for apples. We had so many apples that we gave our slaves what was left over. Ruben always makes sure that our slaves have enough for their families.

We have always stored our apples and other things on the other side of the cellar. We have an English cellar that runs the whole length of the house. We also have a room down here for wines and liquors.

There's another room down here where Miss Betsy and her husband, Larkin, use for weaving and leatherwork. In the winter months Ruben lets Betsy and Larkin live in there. Ruben is good to them. He is good to all our slaves. He's just not good to me! If he was I would not be down here.

It was nice to see Mother and Father when they came to Edmund's celebration. I don't get to see them much anymore. My cousin Isabel and her husband, James Randolph, and their four children came over from Goochland County to spend some time with us.

Isabel and her family spent two nights with us. Mother and Father had to get back to Hanover early the next morning. Father had left my younger brother William in charge of the tavern and inn. I don't think my father had much faith in William. Father did not feel like William could handle things by himself. Father thinks William and Ruben are a lot alike. Father feels like they both talk too much!

The tavern and inn had been given to my mother when

my grandfather died. After my grandfather's death my mother and father had left our family home in the country and had moved into the inn for a while. The inn still sits on the main road to Williamsburg and Richmond, so they do have quite a few guests staying for the night. In fact, Ruben and I lived there for a while.

When Isabel and her family were last here Isabel slept in my room down here in the cellar. Lizzy had made a bed of quilts for me on the floor and Isabel had slept in my bed. I sure hope she was comfortable when she was here.

We talked all night about when we were young girls and she would come over to visit us at Mount Laurel. That's where we met Ruben and James. Ruben lived over at Evergreen and James lived at Poplar Ridge over in Louisa County. I don't think that James was at Mount Laurel but twice.

Isabel and I laughed all night long. At one point Lizzy told us not to be so loud. She said we would wake everyone up upstairs. We had so much fun that night. Isabel got to laughing about the time she took her best quilt outside for her and James to sit on. Isabel's mother was so upset with her.

Isabel had laid the quilt under the huge, beautiful, blooming lilac bush. Isabel's plan must have worked because her and James were married that fall. She said each spring when the lilac is in bloom she will take a bunch of lilac and put it in their room.

I was so sad the morning Isabel had to leave. She was crying and so was I. I looked over at Lizzy and she had tears running down her cheeks and was looking straight down at the ground.

Lizzy would not look at us. When Isabel was leaving the cellar she turned around and looked at me in such a strange way. With tears rolling down her cheeks and with a cracking, soft voice she told me to take care of myself and told me she would be back soon.

Right then I knew I would never see Isabel again. As Lizzy was taking my arm to take me back to my room I watched Isabel walk up the cellar steps and out the door. She never looked back at me.

I lay across my bed all afternoon thinking of all the fun times that Isabel and I had as young girls. She was my sweet cousin and I loved her like a sister. I asked Lizzy did she think Isabel would ever come back to see me.

Lizzy just stared at me in a sad strange way. She said, "Sure, Miss Abigail, Miss Isabel will be back real soon" I knew she was lying! I knew that would never happen. Lizzy told me when I got to feeling better that Miss Isabel would come back. I knew I would never feel better, not living in this cellar.

I miss my sweet cousin! I began to cry and asked over and over and over why they made me stay in the cellar. I was screaming at Lizzy and demanding that she give me an answer. She did not say anything. She just sat there and looked at me like they all do.

I picked up the oil lamp that was sitting on my little table and threw it across the room. When it fell to the ground the oil splattered all over the bottom of Lizzy's dress.

Lizzy jumped up and got off balance and fell to the ground. I started screaming because I did not want Lizzy to be hurt. I only wanted her to answer me! I wanted someone to answer the many questions that I have.

Lizzy ran out of my room and halfway stumbled up the cellar steps on her way out. I knew she was going to get somebody. She always does that when I get very upset. But when she came back she only had a cup of tea with her. I knew that was for me. They had made that kind of tea for me before. It has a smell and does not taste good. I did notice that Lizzy had washed the bottom of her dress because it was still dripping with water.

Lizzy came back with some old rags to clean up the oil. She had one of the young boys with her. He was carrying a pail of water. He was a clumsy sort of boy! I could see the fear on his face as he stumbled down the cellar steps. He did not want to come in here. I could tell.

I did not want to hurt Lizzy. She is so good to me. She is about the only one that cares. I don't know why Lizzy brought that boy down here. All he did was make a mess. The smell of the oil was so sickening I almost threw up Everything almost came up out of my stomach. And my windows are locked so there was no fresh air.

I didn't want to drink that tea cause I knew what it would do to me. But Lizzy stood right there till I drank it all. I must have slept all day and all night, cause when I woke the sun was coming up and I could hear the chopping of wood.

Lizzy had gone out to the kitchen to get me something to eat. I really wasn't hungry, but I'm sure I did eat something. Lizzy does help me so much, so I sure don't want to upset her. But none of them want to listen to me. They don't want to know how I feel. I don't feel like they do. I used to, but not anymore.

Some of the young boys stacked some more wood in my room that morning. They said Mr. Ruben told them it was going to be a very cold day and to make sure Miss Abigail and Lizzy had plenty of firewood. I do love the smell of cedar! I can smell it and think of how it made me feel when I could still go outside.

That was a peaceful time for me. I would not have headaches when I was outside and away from everybody—no screaming children and no one telling me what to do or how to do it. It was so peaceful. They used to ask me so many questions, one question after the other. I hated that!

V
RUBEN'S VISIT

When Ruben and I first met he was so nice looking. I still think he is—well, sometimes anyway. Sometimes when Ruben comes down to the cellar and stays all night with me he tells me I'm still pretty. He usually tells Lizzy she can go for the night and stay with her two boys. Her two boys are almost grown men now. Ruben is real fond of them and will try to have the boys do things around the main house. He does that so they can see their mother almost every day. Lizzy's husband died before I got sick.

Lizzy was sad for a long time, and she never took another man. Last time Ruben stayed the night with me he told me he would have to start going to Williamsburg and Richmond more often. He said he had more business to do there that would take him away from Cedar Grove.

He is always going going going. He's never around here. And when he is here he still does not listen to a word I have to say. I really don't know what he does when he's there, but I'm sure he's talking!

I don't think Ruben likes to be around me anymore. The only time Ruben is nice to me is when he spends the night here in the cellar. He won't ever let me go upstairs and sleep in his bed. He always has one reason or another as to why I cannot go upstairs.

He always says, "Oh I know, Abby, I know." That man doesn't know anything! The only thing he knows is how to stay away from Cedar Grove. He's real good at that.

When Ruben does go to Williamsburg he usually always stays at Father's inn on his way back to Cedar Grove. He enjoys that because there's always other men there who enjoy talking too. I guess they know what they're talking about, but who knows.

Ruben tells me he wants to make things better for Virginia. He needs to make things better for me first! I need help! Don't know what kind but I need something.

If he wanted to he could let me stay in one of the rooms upstairs. That way I could see my children more. Down here in this cellar I hardly get to see anyone anymore. Miss Sally and Chassy come when they can, but they both stay busy.

VI
SMOKING, DRINKING, AND POLITICS

Ruben and I used to have a lot of social gatherings here at Cedar Grove. We would entertain quite often. So much talking and drinking and politics—it seemed that's all the men wanted to do.

And I don't think the men should drink. It seemed like the more they drank the more they talked, one trying to outtalk the other. When they all got together that would go on for hours.

The room was so thick with smoke it would make my head spin, and then I would get sick on my stomach. It took everything I had just to stay in the room. At first I would excuse myself, but later it really didn't matter anymore.

The old men had no idea I was even gone. Every now and then Ruben would ask me why I left the room, and then it got to a point where he didn't even notice. Ruben was so wrapped up in all that mess that the roof could have fallen in and he would have still been talking.

One night after Edmund was born Ruben had a bunch of

old men out to Cedar Grove. It got so loud I felt like my head was going to explode. I had heard them talk about the same old thing for months—nothing new, just the same thing over and over.

I remember pressing my hands to the side of my head in hopes that all the noise would stop. As I was running out the back door I could still hear all the noise and confusion. It was pounding in my head. I was running so fast that I missed the last two steps on the porch and my body fell to the ground.

As I picked myself up I began to scream. I was running straight for the woods. I only had one thing on my mind and that was to get out of that house and into the woods. Things seemed to change in my mind. I felt confused, frustrated, and really felt like I didn't know what I was doing. No one would listen to me. I felt like they didn't want to hear me, that they did not want to hear how I felt. It's like everybody would upset me, especially my children.

It seemed like I was in the woods for a few hours, but I was not afraid. As I was walking back to the house I ran into Uncle Pete and Old Joe. Uncle Pete hollered out at me in a voice I had not heard before: "Why are you out here, Miss Abigail? It's dark and you know things come out at night. And Mr. Ruben had to excuse himself from his men folks to try to find you. Now Miss Abigail, you know that ain't right. Now come on so we can get back to the house. It's late and you've got everyone worried.

As we got back to the back steps there stood Sally shaking her head and looking straight at me. And about that time

Ruben rounded the corner of the house with Benson right behind him. Ruben got right in my face and said, "My god, Abby, what in the world has come over you? Have you totally lost your mind! Something has got to change, Abby. There is no excuse for this, Abigail!"

Ruben told me how upset he was and that I had taken him away from his guests. He told me how important they where and that I knew nothing about that sort of thing. Then he demanded that I go in the house; he'd had enough of me for one night.

Before Ruben put me in the cellar he would talk terrible to me. It was almost like he would dismiss me when he was through talking to me. I've got news for that old goat! I'm not one of his slaves that he can dismiss when he is through talking. Who does he think he is!

Uncle Pete and Miss Sally took me right to my room that night. Ruben made sure that no one was around as we passed through the hallway. Ruben was looking all around to make sure no one caught a glimpse of me as we passed. I guess he's ashamed of me. I don't remember much about that night. My mind was so tired that I couldn't think straight. I guess Ruben went back to his guests. No telling how long they all stayed.

When I woke up the next morning Ruben was standing over me staring right through me. As I opened my eyes he looked me over from head to toe. He had a terrible frown on his face and looked like he wanted to say something. But he did not.

He did not move; he just stood there staring at me. I

remember being a little afraid, not knowing what was going to happen. I don't believe I had ever seen Ruben with that look on his face.

He did not talk to me for the rest of the day. In fact, when I entered the room he would leave. I told him I did not care how he acted. I also told him I did not like all that drinking and talking. A bunch of old men flapping their jaws! He just turned around and walked out of the room.

VII

JUDITH ANNE

Oh, I remember my sweet Judith Anne when she was a little girl. She is my oldest child. She was born when we lived at Mount Laurel. Ruben and I lived there for a while with my mother and father before moving to Louisa County. Then, later, Ruben bought Cedar Grove.

Miss Sally used to help me with my babies because I sure didn't know anything about them. I think Judy Anne has always been my best child. She always wanted to help with her younger brother and sisters, and she did a good job too.

When Miss Sally and I were doing other things she would watch the younger children. Miss Sally, Betsy, Larkin, and Ben were all part of my marriage dowry. Ben, bless his heart, and Larkin would help Ruben farm the land.

The first few years of our marriage were hard. Ruben and I were so much in love, but it seemed like when one thing went wrong so did ten others. Our first tobacco crop failed, but it was a terrible drought that year so I can't blame Ruben. Ruben, Larkin, and Ben all worked as hard as they could. Ruben would come in at night with his hands cracked and blistered. Some nights his hands would bleed.

We did try one more year with tobacco, but that crop was not good either. Ruben did not have any experience with labor. That is something that he's never been good at. So Ruben decided to buy a store and sell all kinds of merchandise. He did well, I guess, but that was because he likes to talk to people.

The store sat right on the road to Williamsburg. That is a busy road, so I'm sure that helped, and it wasn't too far from my father's tavern and inn. And the Hanover courthouse is also in the area. That gave Ruben another chance to do more talking and meet more people. Ruben told me more than once that he enjoyed talking about what was going on in Virginia and how he hoped things would change. I really did not know what he was talking about but I think he did.

Ruben used to tell me that when he and other men would get together that they would talk about how they could change Virginia. He would always say, "Believe me, Abby, things will get better for Virginia—you just wait and see."

Sweet Judith Anne looks more like my mother, but she has raven-black hair like me and my father. All my brothers and sisters have black hair and black eyes, and four out of my six children have black hair and black eyes. My other two children look more like Ruben's family. In fact, my Madison looks more like Ruben's father.

When Judith Anne married we had Chassy make her a beautiful dress. She got married right after we moved here. She married her second cousin Randolph Bacon from over in Louisa County. Judith Anne met Randolph at a social gathering at her grandfather Lewis's plantation one fall.

Sometimes Judith Anne and her son Henry come and stay a week with me. When she comes, me and Lizzy enjoy her company so much. She's always been so much fun to be with. When she is here she will sleep here in the cellar with me.

I remember that on one of her visits Ruben let me and Lizzy eat upstairs with my family, but that did not last long. Ruben put a stop to all that. He said that would never happen again! The last time I ate upstairs with my children was a sad and terrible day. The children were so noisy and rowdy. Ruben would not control them at all. He just let them do whatever they wanted without any concern for how I was feeling. My head was pounding within the first five minutes of being in the room with all that noise.

I could not believe what I was seeing. Each time I would try to correct one of them Ruben would jump in and tell me I was imagining things. He told me everything was in my head. At one point Ruben said, "There you go again, Abby!"

Then Ruben started screaming at me for no reason at all. Then he told me "What is it with you, woman? You act like you've lost all your senses!"

That hurt me so much when Ruben said that. It hurt me to the bone. It was as if he had spit in my face. How could someone who supposedly loves you talk to you like that? And in front of everybody in the room!

And that Catherine Louise, I don't know what was wrong with her. She continued to knock on the floor with the chair leg, and she was old enough to know that was wrong. That is just pure bad manners. It seemed like the noise was getting louder and louder each time I heard that chair leg hit the wood floor.

After a while I got so upset that I grabbed Catherine Louise's plate and threw it on the floor with her food still on it. At that moment Ruben pounded the table with his fist, shaking everything on the table and screaming at me all at the same time. Then he started screaming at me again. Ruben yelled out, "What in God's name is wrong with you, Abigail?"

Before Ruben could get his hands on me I quickly grabbed his plate and threw it against the wall. Then I turned around and picked up the pitcher of water from the table and threw it as hard as I could across the room. With water all over the floor, Ruben was still trying to make his way to me.

Ruben yelled for Lizzy and Madison to do something with me. Seemed like they both just stood there, probably not knowing what to do at that point. Then it seemed like Lizzy and Madison both grabbed me and held me the best they could as Ruben was reaching for some cloth on the table.

Somehow Ruben got the cloth and quickly tied my hands together. I was screaming and kicking at them with everything I had, but I could not break away. They had me where I could hardly move.

It seemed like Ruben got more cloth from the table, but before he could stuff it in my mouth I began biting Ruben on the shoulder. When I looked up, Madison was crying like a baby. I don't remember seeing the other children at that point. I guess Sally had walked in and taken them to another part of the house. But I do remember Judith Anne begging her father to please not take me back to the cellar.

I'm sure Ruben did not even hear her. Ruben continued screaming my name as he tried to grab my legs and hold them together. He kept yelling, "Abigail, you have upset the children once again and only God knows what I'm going to do with you." Somehow I do remember at some point seeing Ruben's face. He had tears running down his cheeks and his hands were trembling as he tried to tie my legs together.

Somehow they got me back to the cellar. Madison and Lizzy laid me across my bed as Ruben tightly tucked my bed linens under me. I guess he thought that would keep me in the bed. Sally was right behind him with a bowl of cool water for my face and head.

The cool water felt good as Sally softly bathed my face. I remember feeling so strange that afternoon. I was having feelings that I did not have when I was living upstairs. It was the strangest thing. I was so weak after all of that happened. I heard Lizzy tell Sally that she had to get out of the cellar for a while.

Lizzy and Sally were trying to talk softly, but I could still hear most of what they were saying. I know I did hear Lizzy say that she did not know if she could take much more. I don't know what she really meant by that.

I feel that way too! I can't take much more! And me not being able to see my children breaks my heart. Those are my babies and I love them. Why does Ruben make me and Lizzy stay in this cellar?

The next morning as the sun was coming up Judith Anne brought me something to eat. She said she had to go back to her home and take care of some things. She told me she had been here six or seven days, but I don't believe her! There's no way she's been here that long. I might get confused sometimes, but I'm not crazy like they all think I am. I know that's what they all think. They don't come out and say it, but that's what they think.

Judith Anne was smiling at me when she told me she would be back as soon as she could. I could hear Madison and Old Joe hitching up the wagon to take her to the stagecoach inn down the road a few miles.

As she was walking up the cellar steps she turned around, and with tears running down her cheeks she blew me a kiss and said, "I love you, Mother."

To hear the wagon get farther and farther down the road broke my heart. I listened for the last turn of the wagon wheel, and then everything was quiet. My sweet Judith Anne was gone.

VIII
ALL NIGHT

My God, I guess I've sat here all night thinking, thinking about how things used to be and how things are now. I don't like how things are now. Everything is gone! I don't have anything. I want to sneak out, but I think I have to wait because it's too late. There seems to be a chill in the air tonight. I still have a small fire, but that's going to burn out soon. Lizzy will probably be waking up soon to get a good fire going again. It sure looks like dawn is almost here. Maybe it's best that I don't go out tonight since it's so late. Maybe they will leave my door unlocked again. I sure hope so.

I will check tonight to see if Lizzy has forgotten to bolt my door again. I don't know; Lizzy doesn't forget much. And if Ruben ever found out there's no telling what would happen. He would be so upset with Lizzy.

I forget sometimes how long I've been in the cellar. Lizzy says two years now, but I couldn't tell you. I know little Edmund is over two years old now. I got real sad and started thinking real strange and weird things shortly after I birthed Edmund.

I knew things were not right. I had never felt that way after birthing any of my other children. Things just all changed, and

I don't even know why. I could never talk to Ruben, because he was gone so much. And he still is. I don't know what in the world that man does while he is away.

I felt like everybody wanted so much from me: my children, Ruben, my mother and father, and the slaves too. Really just about everyone. Always questions. Questions questions questions. It never ended! If it wasn't one person it was the other. No one ever understood me. I don't think they want to. When I first got sad, I would go riding by myself. I liked to go riding in the backwoods far away from everyone. Ruben would tell me I would feel a lot better after a nice ride. Ruben never tells me the truth about anything. He didn't then and he still doesn't.

He lies to me, like all the rest of them do. He would always say that I was gone way too long on my rides. He would act like everyone was worried about me. With him being gone most of the time, how in the world would he know what goes on around here?

He could stay with me sometimes, if he wanted to. He doesn't have to be gone so much. When I would go riding, Sally would always watch the children. She's always been good with my children. They love her and so do I. I really liked not being with the children so much. That way I did not have to listen to them.

There was always something that the children wanted from me. And it was always one question after the other. The things that the children would do was enough to make me scream. And I did! It seemed as if it was all day long, nonstop—especially

the younger children. It seemed like all I was doing was screaming and crying.

I do like being alone without the children. That way they
won't bother me. Sometimes I would get so angry with them
that I felt like taking a hickory stick to their backsides. I never
did, but I sure felt like it sometimes. Because I do love them,
it's just they bother me so much. I just don't know why they
won't do what I want them to do.

I do remember one time that I did want so badly to take a
hickory stick after that old Miss Elizabeth Carr. She had stopped
by here unexpected and unwanted. She lives over at Chatham
Hill, not too far away from here—close enough that she came by
herself in her wagon, just her. She was a tough old bird!

There were times she would stop by and would talk about
things that were of no interest to me. She would babble on and
on about everything. It didn't matter what it was, she always
had an opinion. I didn't like her then and I sure don't now.

Miss Sally would always tell me not to pay any attention to
what she had to say. Sally would tell me, "Just use your manners,
Miss Abigail, and then don't pay her no mind." That was hard to
do since the woman was saying things that would upset me.

She had never married and was always trying to tell people
how and what to do. She stopped by one afternoon when I
was still living upstairs and the minute she walked in the door
those eyes of hers began looking all around the room. I never
could understand what she was looking at or looking for. I
don't think she knew herself. She never had to work for anything in her life. Her grandfather had built Chatham Hill, so

she always had the finer things. She never knew what it was like to struggle. She never knew what it was like to have a husband and slaves that would have bloody hands at the end of the day because of their hard work.

I know on one of her visits she had brought an apple cake for the children, and she had a bunch of flowers in her other hand for me. And if the truth was known, she probably had picked the flowers out of my flower garden. I do have one that's at the end of the road before you make the turn. I used to love to walk down there and work in that flower garden. It was away from the house and away from the children. It was peaceful—nobody but me and my flowers.

Uncle Pete had some of the boys dig that flower garden for me. He was real proud of it because it had flowers in almost every season. Sometimes I would walk down there with Uncle Pete, but mostly by myself. I don't know if anyone tends that garden or not anymore. Probably not, because nobody seems to care what goes on around here now.

As soon as Miss Carr's wagon rounded the bend in the road and was out of sight, I took that apple cake and gave it to Benson. I told him to throw it to the hogs. I'm sure he ate some of it before doing that. But that's okay; that was all right. I just did not want that thing in my house. And as far as the flowers go, I threw them as hard as I could out the front door. No telling what she had put in that cake!

And I dared that Ruben to say a word to me about that. Sally was standing there, but she did not say a word. She looked at me with a funny look, but she did not say a word.

IX
DAYBREAK

I hear the rooster! I'm glad I did not sneak out. I would have gotten caught for sure. I hear Lizzy stirring around, so won't be long before she will be in here. I guess Lizzy is getting ready for the day. I need to get back in bed so she won't know I've been up all night.

Sure enough, in a matter of minutes Lizzy is right at my bed asking me how I slept. I turn over as if I had been asleep, but I think Lizzy knows something has been going on.

Lizzy always wants to dress me as soon as we wake. I don't like doing that! There's no need for that. I'm not going anywhere. I never get to go anywhere. So why do I have to get dressed every morning?

I like sitting around in my shift. There's nothing to do anyway. There's nothing in this cellar, and no one ever comes to visit me. The children every now and then, but that's not often. I just sit here, day in and day out, staring at the cellar walls. What a life!

There is a chill in the air, so I wrap my shoulders with my shawl that Chassy made me last Christmas. Catherine Louise made me a nice one too. These Virginia winter days are always cold. It doesn't seem like you ever get warm the whole winter, especially down here in the cellar. It's always cold down here. Even in the summer sometimes there's a dampness in the air down here. Ruben doesn't care, but you can bet he is warm!

"I'll have Benson or one of the boys bring in some more wood, because it sure looks like we will need a good fire all day. As cold as it is I think that would be good," Lizzy says.

Lizzy is good to me, and takes good care of me. When Lizzy gets back with my food she just stands there staring at the floor. She doesn't say a word. She just stands there. I ask her what is wrong, but she does not answer.

Later, she tells me that Belle told Ettie that she was with child, and Belle told Benson that she did not want to marry. Lizzy says she had heard that Ruben had talked to Belle last week and that he had promised her that if she was to marry he would never sell her, her baby, or Benson.

Poor Lizzy, I feel so sorry for her. She looks so worried about Belle and the baby. Lizzy always wants to do the right thing. I tell her if that's what Ruben said, then he will stick to his word, and she's knows he is a man of his word.

I want to get some sleep because I was up all night, but Lizzy does not know that. She kind of raises her voice at me when I tell her I want to go back to bed. Then she starts with the questions: one question after the other.

I tell her I want to be alone and get some rest, and I don't want to talk to anybody anymore about anything. Then she starts telling me that I get too much rest and that I need to start walking around more to get my blood flowing right. Well, only so much walking around you can do when you live in the cellar. I am so upset with Lizzy. She knows we hardly get to get out of this cellar. She knows that! Why would she say something crazy like that to me.

I ask Lizzy to check with Sally to see if Sarah is feeling better. I know she had the croup and some fever the other day. That remedy that Sally always uses really works; I don't know what is in there, but must be some powerful stuff.

Lizzy tells me something about how Sarah was sick last month. She says she was feeling better but that was weeks ago. I told her I did not know what she was talking about. I know Sally told me that my girl was sick. I don't know what the woman told Lizzy. They all must be mixed up, because she sure told me my girl was sick.

"Oh my God, Lizzy, for God's sake, will you please go on and do whatever you were going to do. Just go! You're bothering me, Lizzy! Go on and get out of here. I mean it, Lizzy!"

I like Lizzy, but my God she upsets me so much when she just keeps telling me stuff over and over and over. I want them to leave me alone.

Before I got sick Sarah and I would read together. I think she likes to read as much as I do. That Ruben needs to bring me some more books. I'm always asking him to bring me a new book from Williamsburg, but I'm still waiting on that book.

No one knows how terrible it is down here in the cellar. I know it's hard for Lizzy too, but she never says anything about it. I guess she just thinks this is how it is and goes on. Well, I can't do that. I can't go on like this. I do not have any kind of life: no family, no children, nothing to look forward to. I'm just waiting to die.

X

DR. DUKE

"Miss Abigail, Martha Elizabeth and Catherine Louise want to come down here today after schooling to see you. Do you feel like visiting with them for a little while? They miss you and love you very much. Last time they were down here for a visit you got real ugly with Martha Elizabeth. You said something about her dress that made her cry, and I don't think she's been down here since then. You said something about the color looking bad."

"Well, I don't know about all that, but anyway it probably was the wrong color and I don't want my child wearing some bad color."

"Please Miss Abigail, don't upset the children again, please. Sarah has made some pretty fall things for you. She got some pretty leaves and picked out a pumpkin right out of the south garden. And she brought it up to the house all by herself. Won't that be nice, Miss Abigail?"

"Oh I don't know, Lizzy! Don't be talking to me about so many things all at once. Just let all of them do whatever they want. They will do it anyway. I'm so tired and I don't want to talk anymore. So go on, Lizzy, and let me be."

"Why do you have to talk so ugly, Miss Abigail? Those babies upstairs haven't done anything wrong, and they don't know what's going on. All they know is their mother does not live upstairs with them anymore. They don't know why you live in the cellar and we do not know why you live in the cellar.

Lizzy I can tell you one thing, all of you are good at talking and doing things to upset me. You people need to leave me alone. All of you need to tend to your own selves and stop upsetting me. I don't care what the children do; just don't upset me. All of you say things that don't make a whole lot of sense. It's got to where I don't understand half of what y'all are talking about, and I don't think y'all do either!"

"Miss Abigail I'll get you ready later so we can sit outside with those babies for a while this afternoon. They will like that and so will you! You just think you won't like it, but you will. I see Miss Sally had Lawrence sit out some chairs and a small table under a big tree. I see Sarah has put her pretty things on the table. Maybe it will be nice to get out for a while. It looks like a little breeze, but the fresh air will be nice I guess."

The warmth from the sun feels good on us. Lizzy and I are both wearing a shawl, which feels good on a fall day. It is enough to knock the chill off.

My Sarah is getting so tall, and every time I see her she looks more like Ruben's sister. All the Lewises are pretty people. It looks like my Sarah will become a beautiful woman. And I think Martha Elizabeth is sweet on Joseph Lee over at Cherry Hill.

But she never talks to me about him. I haven't seen much

of that boy since he was a little guy, but I know he is from a good family and that sure means a lot. I have never known a Lee that was not good: good blood and good manners.

We sit partly facing the south so the afternoon sun will warm us. Sarah tells Miss Sally she wants to bring out some special cups for our hot apple cider. As Lizzy and I sit with the girls I can't help but think of how it was before I got sick. I love my children and it breaks my heart not to be able to be with them.

I wish I could remember everything that happened that afternoon, but sometimes it's hard for me to remember anything. I think it's cause I stay so upset. I do remember wanting to stay out and enjoy the outdoors more that afternoon because it passed by so quickly.

But that afternoon I did walk to the front of the house when Lizzy was playing with Sarah and Martha Elizabeth had gone to the kitchen to get more apple cider. It had been years since I had been in the front of the house. Things did not look the same. Someone had recently trimmed the old boxwoods that were beside the front porch, and someone had planted a new bed of periwinkle on the other side of the boxwoods. They were such a bright pink color. They were beautiful. I used to love to work in my herb garden. Sometimes Uncle Pete would help me with some of the planting of seeds. He said it helped his mind too. It was a beautiful garden. When we first moved here to Cedar Grove, Ruben had bought me some seeds from Williamsburg and they did well the first year. I always saved my seeds cause I did not know if I would ever get anymore.

I remember walking down the path between the two rows of cedars that run not far from the boxwoods. The cedars go all the way to the road. I was thinking back about when we first moved to Cedar Grove. Ruben had named our plantation Cedar Grove cause I loved the smell of cedar so much. We were so happy back then.

I felt good and so alive; I did not feel so alone, as I do now. Ruben has always been gone so much, but that did not bother me back then. I had the children and could do things around here that I enjoyed. I feel like it's just me now, alone and waiting to die. Why do they think the cellar is where I should live?

I don't want to live anymore. I don't have a life or anything to look forward to each day. I hate people! I hate the way they make me feel. I try to tell them how I feel, but they don't listen. And that Dr. Duke is nothing but a bag of hot air! He has bled me a time or two and I sure did not like it. I begged Ruben to please not let him do that to me again. It just made me weaker than I already was.

Ruben did have a cousin over in Louisa County that they had bled some years back, and that poor old soul never got out of bed again. He died before the night was over. He had the fever or something.

And there have been a few times that some men from the church over in Hanover have come out here and tied me to my bed and placed a cross on my forehead. I was so scared that I wet all over myself. Lizzy or Ruben, either one, stayed in the room with me when they were doing all of that.

At one point I did see Sally peep around the corner of my

door, but when I looked again she was gone. As they were tying me to my bed they were saying things I had never heard before. I was so afraid and alone. Nobody was there with me, not even my Lizzy.

I was screaming and kicking all of them, but they were so much stronger than I was. Two of the men were almost sitting on me while the other one was tying me to the bed. At some point before they got started one of them was mixing something up in a cup. Two of them were holding my head while the other one almost poured the drink down my throat.

I remember one time they pressed the cross so hard on my forehead that it broke the skin. I kept telling them it was hurting, but they did not stop. Lizzy had to put some salve on my forehead. It was sore for days.

I cried that afternoon as I walked down the path, thinking of how much I hated being alone. I hated the thought of living in the cellar. I started beating the palms of my hands against a cedar tree until they bled. The more I cried the more I beat my hands

I remember falling to my knees and screaming, screaming until my throat was raw. Then I got to my feet and started running. I didn't know where I was going, but I just had to run. I got as far as the creek before I twisted my ankle. After that I could not run anymore, or even walk. I lay there on the ground hoping I would die. I wanted all of this to be over.

I didn't want to live anymore—not like I had been living, living in the cellar of my house, not able to see my children or any of my family. Ruben had taken all of that away from me when he put me in the cellar.

Ruben had taken my life away. He had put me in a lonely dungeon that was cold, damp, and where not much sun could shine through my windows. I hate Ruben for doing that to me. Does Ruben hate me that much!

As I lay on the ground I started thinking about Dr. Duke again. That man upsets me every time I think about him. He's always telling Ruben a bunch of lies

about me. I hate both of them. Ruben is always right outside the cellar door waiting for the old man to come out.

If Lizzy is not watching me I will stand on a chair and press my ear against the wall hoping I can hear what the two of them have to say about me. But the walls are so thick down there I can never hear anything.

But one day before Lizzy bolted my door I did hear Dr. Duke tell Reuben that he thought I had gone crazy. He said he thought I was a danger to myself and others. I could not hear what Ruben said cause Lizzy had already closed the door.

I know what I heard the old man say. Well, I got news for him and Ruben too: I'm not crazy! I get mixed up sometimes, but I'm not crazy.

And then another time Ruben had walked in before Dr. Duke left my room and they started talking. It was something about a new place over in Williamsburg that could take care of people like me. What in God's name did he mean by that!

What did he mean people like me! They walked out and I could hear Ruben bolt the door before they left the cellar.

After I heard that I ran across the room grabbed my candle

holder from my little table and began to knock the glass out of my locked windows. I kept beating on the glass until it shattered.

Ruben quickly ran back to my room and started screaming for Lizzy. By the time Lizzy got there I had knocked out two of my windows. Lizzy quickly jerked my bed linens off my bed while Ruben and Dr. Duke held me where I could not move.

I was screaming at Ruben, telling him how much I hated him for keeping me in the cellar. None of them said a word. After Lizzy had stripped my bed, Ruben and Dr. Duke forced me to lie flat on the bed.

Ruben sat on my chest and held my arms up while Lizzy and Dr. Duke tied my hands to the bedpost. Ruben quickly raised my dress and tore a piece of my cotton shift off and stuffed it in my mouth.

With tears running down Ruben's cheeks he took both his hands and placed them around my face and softly said, "Oh my sweet Abby, I am so sorry." Then he quickly jumped off my chest and ran out my door.

With everything going on I could still hear what sounded like Ruben stumbling his way up the cellar steps and out into the yard. Dr. Duke stood there for a few more minutes just staring at me. He never said a word to me, he just kept looking at me. He finally left and bolted the door behind him.

Lizzy just stood there like a chunk of rock staring at me. She pulled her chair close to me and sat with me, but never said a word. She just sat there watching me with no expression on her face.

After a while she did leave for a few minutes and came back with some cool water and a cloth. She bathed my face for what seemed like a long time. But she still never spoke. I remember her telling me that she was sick to her stomach and that she was going to have to leave the cellar for a few minutes. I remember when I woke up the next morning the sun was glaring through the shattered glass in my windows.

I was in so much pain as I lay on the ground wanting to die. I could tell my ankle was swelling more and more. I knew I could not walk with all this pain I was feeling. Then I begin to think how upset Ruben will be when he came back from Williamsburg tonight. The sun was beginning to set and I knew there was no way I could walk back to the house.

XI
LET ME DIE

As I lay there I kept thinking of my children and my life without them. I don't have a life anymore. Ruben and his mother have taken all of that away from me. She needs to keep herself away from Cedar Grove. Nobody wants her around here. All she ever does when she does come is cause problems for every body. Everything that woman says, Ruben usually does.

I don't care if Ruben is mad at me when he gets back tonight. All I want is peace, and I won't have any till I die. I think that is what Ruben wants anyway. Well, maybe it won't be too long.

Somehow I was able to crawl to the water, knowing this time of year the creek would be full and cold. When I reached the water I put my ankle and half of my leg in the cold water, hoping some of the swelling would stop. My whole body was now aching. I washed the dried blood from my hands and arms. I thought if they would just let me out of the cellar this would not have happened.

Why don't they want me to be happy! I don't understand and I never understood. They all like it if I'm upset. Oh no, I bet Ruben will try to tie me to the bedpost again tonight when he gets back.

I sat on the creek bank trembling with every breath I took. I was shaking so much my breathing had become hard. My whole body was shaking. I could not stand the water anymore, so I took my ankle and leg from the water hoping for some relief.

I tried to get warm by pulling my knees and legs up close to my chest. I covered them with the bottom of my dress.

Oh no, I have gotten my new pretty dress so dirty! Look at what I've done! Chassy will be so upset with me. She will never make me anything else. I am so sorry, Chassy, for what I've done. Please forgive me!

As evening began to fall I could feel the night air against my chilled body. I was so cold. I began to cry and scream, knowing how upset Ruben would be with me if I didn't get back before he did. All I could think about was how to get warm. I knew if I did not get warm soon that I would get the chills and maybe die and no one would know where I was.

All I could think about was my children and how happy I was at one time in my life. I remember the day that Ruben asked my father if he could marry me. Ruben was so nervous that afternoon when he rode up to Mount Laurel. And to make things worse, my father was sitting on the front porch waiting for him. Of course Ruben did not know that I had already talk to my father. I wanted to let my father know that Ruben would be coming.

Ruben was so nervous that when he got off his horse he got

off balance and almost fell to the ground. I saw it all from my upstairs bedroom window. I had been up there all afternoon knowing Ruben was coming. Why isn't it like that anymore! Why are there no days that I can laugh and giggle as I did on that day and many, many days to follow?

All of a sudden I thought I heard the creaking of a wagon wheel, and it was not far away. I screamed out for Lizzy, but there was no answer. I screamed, "Old Joe, Old Joe!" I screamed I'm over here! I'm over by the creek bank." Then I heard Madison shout, "Mother, where are you!" I screamed out Madison's name as loud as I could. I screamed that I was over on the east side of the creek.

As the wagon got closer to me I could see Lizzy, Old Joe, and Madison coming up the path toward me. Madison yelled out, "Don't move, Mother, stay where you are and we will come to you!" When they got to me I was shaking so hard I could not speak. Madison and Old Joe jumped out of the wagon and rushed toward me as Lizzy was grabbing for a quilt.

Lizzy quickly wrapped the quilt around my cold body as I lay there not knowing if I was able to move. I felt as if the cold water from the creek had frozen my whole body. I could not move.

As Madison and Old Joe begin to pick me up I screamed. I told them I had hurt my ankle and could not walk. My whole body was in pain. I remember crying and crying because I was hurting so much. They laid me in the back of the wagon and put some more quilts on me, trying to keep me as warm as they could. I remember asking Madison if his father was home yet.

Madison did not answer me.

Madison really scolded me about leaving the house. He asked me why I ran off. He said that everyone was so worried about me and the girls were very upset. He told me Ruben would be very upset with me when he found out what I had done. I told Madison I just wanted to get away for a while. Madison was very upset with me, and that got me upset, and I asked Madison what difference it made cause he spends all his time over at Lotus Grove.

I think I hurt Madison's feelings. Then he got to talking about Jane or something, I don't know. I was hurting so bad I could not even think. That boy has been going over to Lotus Grove for no telling how long now.

When we got back to the house Old Joe jumped out of the wagon and opened the cellar door while Madison carried me inside. I was still chilled to the bone. I started crying because I did not want to go back to the cellar. I begged Madison to take me upstairs and put me in another room. I could see tears in his eyes, but he would not talk to me. He finally said, "I cannot do that, Mother."

As Madison carried me to my bed Lizzy quickly began to build a fire to try to warm me. Madison wrapped my ankle, hoping that would help the swelling. I don't remember too much after that, but I do remember somebody brought me some hot tea. I'm sure it was the kind that Sally makes, the kind that will put you to sleep and you will sleep all night.

I do barely remember Madison kissing me on my cheek

and covering me with a quilt. I had begun to get so sleepy, but I could still feel the pain in my ankle and leg. Madison kissed me again and gave me a hug and told me he would see me the next day.

XII
OUR FALL FEAST

As I woke the next morning I could still feel the pain in my body. It seemed as if everything was hurting, and now the palms of my hands had begun to swell. I wanted to get out of bed but I could not. Everything was hurting!

Lizzy kept putting more wood in the fire, hoping that would help me some, but it did not. She told me she was going to the kitchen to get us something to eat. I did not feel like eating, but maybe I did. I kept staring out my window hoping the sunlight would help.

When Lizzy got back she told me that it was time for our fall feast again. She said the boys had been busy dressing and smoking wild turkeys. She said Ruben had told her that he had the boys fattening up the turkeys for us. Ruben told Miss Sally that everybody had worked very hard this year getting in all the crops for a good harvest and everything else that had to be done here on the plantation.

Ruben has been saying he was real proud of everybody. He told me that a few weeks ago. Ruben was proud of our crops too.

We always try to have enough meat for each family, as well

as potatoes. Lizzy told me that we had enough potatoes this year to feed two plantations. We had white potatoes and good old sweet potatoes. Boy, I sure do like sweet potatoes! So it looks like there will be a number of baskets left over for the slaves, and there will be plenty of greens and turnips through part of the winter. Greens are always better after we've had a good frost on the ground—such good eating.

Chassy made me another dress for our fall feast. She told me if I got any thinner I'd be wearing Catherine Louise's dresses. I don't like eating anymore. I don't think it's that good, but I can't help that. It makes me sick to my stomach sometimes and it comes back up. It's the same old thing every day. Everything has changed since I've been living in the cellar.

This is a cold dungeon of a place. Sometimes it feels as if there is no fire at all. Sally, or maybe it's Lizzy, tells me I'm cold because my blood is not moving like it was before. Well, I know that, because there's nothing for me to do down here. I'm just down here, that's all.

Lizzy and I do not have a wood or stone floor down here. It's just dirt. I heard Lizzy one day tell Reuben that he needed to put some stones down in the cellar. She told him it was just too cold for us. Lizzy did catch a death of a cold last March and was sick for weeks, but Ruben does not seem to care how we feel. Just as long as he's warm and cozy that's all that matters to him. I'm sure he still has Sally or Benson put hot coals under his bed on these cold winter nights. Lizzy tells me that I should not think things like that, cause they are not true! She says Ruben does care about how we feel.

That Lawrence was down here this morning and he had about as much sense as a goose. I don't know about that boy. I don't think he's all there. I told him to put my wood on the other side of the room, but he doesn't listen either. But after I picked up a hickory stick and popped him across his back and legs he began to listen.

That boy started hollering. I'm sure you could have heard him halfway across the fields. Then he started screaming and asking me what was wrong with me! I told that boy there was nothing wrong with me! About that time Lizzy ran into the room screaming for me to stop. She was screaming, telling me to stop beating up on Lawrence.

I told her they don't listen to me anymore. They don't listen to a word I say. I told her that boy didn't have any sense and that's why I popped him across his legs. I also told Lizzy that boy was ugly. Lizzy just looked at me like she does so much and did not say a word.

Later she told me that was just devil talk and told me to stop saying ugly things to people. Lizzy was very upset with me. It seems like she is always trying to tell me what to do.

I got very upset with Lizzy one time. I had asked her to do something and she paid me no mind. She just kept doing whatever she was doing. I grabbed her arm to get her attention and she quickly broke from me. She went running up the cellar steps and out to the back.

I looked out my window and saw Lizzy crying. I saw her running as hard as she could toward Old Joe. He was out back chopping wood. He quickly dropped the ax and they both started running back to the cellar.

I knew what they were thinking. They thought they were going to tie me to the bed again. If they do I'll tell Ruben and he will make sure they don't do that again. Oh, Ruben doesn't care anymore. He doesn't care how I'm treated. He wants them to treat me bad. I know he thinks I deserve it.

But I don't deserve it and I don't deserve to live in this cellar. They wouldn't tie me up this time! I quickly ran back to my bed and pulled off the bed linens. I twisted some of them around my arm and grabbed a piece of burning wood from the fire. I pressed the burning wood against the bed linen until it began to blaze.

By this time Lizzy and Old Joe had made their way to my room. When they saw the linen burning around my arm Old Joe quickly grabbed me up and threw me across his shoulder and took me outside. As soon as we made it out of the cellar Old Joe pushed me to the ground, trying to smother the fire out.

I could hear Lizzy screaming to the Lord as she was trying to put out the fire I had also started on my quilt. By this time I did not know what was happening. It felt as if my head was spinning. The next thing I knew Benson had run up after hearing Lizzy screaming. Old Joe tried to pick me up after he had put out the fire, but he was having a hard time cause I was screaming and kicking with all my strength. Somehow the both of them got me up off the ground, but I began crying and biting Benson's shoulder, so it was hard for them to hold me.

Somehow they got me to Old Joe's cabin, dragging me part

of the way. I was screaming and demanding that they let me go. I wanted them to get their filthy hands off of me. I was begging Lizzy to please make them stop and to take me back to the cellar. Lizzy stood there with her face wet with tears and never said a word. She never looked at me as they were dragging me up the steps of Old Joe's cabin.

I started wetting all over myself. I could feel it running down my thighs and on down my legs. Benson held me as Old Joe began tying me to the cane chair. Old Joe kept saying, "Please, Lord, take the devil out of this child. Lord, this child is not right in her mind. Please, Lord, this sickness is rotting her mind."

Lizzy quickly dropped to her knees and began praying. She kept saying the same words over and over. She was begging the Lord to make all of this stop. She was praying to the Lord and telling him that none of us can go on like this. At one point she was screaming my name and telling the Lord that my mind was gone.

As Benson bent down to wipe the tears from my face with a wet cloth I spit in his face and demanded again that they untie me. Lizzy's trembling body was rocking back and forth as she sat on the floor staring at me. But she did not come close to me; she kept her distance. Old Joe tried to get close to me to wipe my face, but as he did I tried to bite his hand.

Then all of them just stood there motionless, not knowing what to do at that point. It seemed the more I cried and tried to twist around in the chair the more the rope twisted around my wrists.

Madison must have heard me screaming as he was riding up to the house. I don't know where he had been, but all of a sudden he burst through the door of the cabin. The boy's face was as white as snow. He fell to his knees in front of me and cried like a child.

He told me he was going to ride and get Dr. Duke. I remember telling Madison that if people would just listen to what I have to say things like this would not happen. I told him I did not want to look at his face any longer and to get out.

The boy did not know what to say, but he told me that I could not go on like this and that he was afraid that I was going to hurt someone or hurt myself. He cut the rope from my wrists that were raw from me twisting them. He told me that Ruben would be home shortly and that I would have to answer to him.

I told Madison that I was not afraid of his father and I would take care of him. Madison asked me what in the world was I thinking when I set fire to the bed linens.

Sally had brought me another cup of whatever she usually brings me to drink when I get up so upset. They never tell me what's in the cup, and I hate the taste of it! I did not want to drink it and I told them so. Old Joe and Benson held my head while Madison poured it down my throat.

I don't remember them taking me back to the cellar. I just remember the next morning and the smell of burnt cloth. It was so strong it was sickening. A few times I felt as if I was going to throw up. It was a horrible smell.

Lizzy does not leave the cellar much anymore, and when she does I can always hear her bolt that door. They sure stare at me all the time now. No one hardly talked to me before, but they sure don't now. They just look at me.

XIII
MORE LIES

I'm so cold I'm shaking, but I can smell the cedar from the fireplace so I know there is a fire. I can hear Lizzy stirring around in my room, but I'm confused. What is happening! I can barely hear Lizzy calling my name.

"Ruben, is that you?"

"Yes, Abby, I'm here. I'm here with you. Abby, do you remember anything that has happened?" asked Ruben.

"No, what's happened? Where is Lizzy!"

"Everybody is here, Abigail, so don't you worry about anything. You just get some rest and try not to worry about things. I'm going to sit with you till you fall back to sleep. Now close your eyes and don't think about anything," said Ruben.

I was getting sleepy again, but did not want to sleep because I was so confused. I could feel Ruben softly touching my face, something that he had not done in a very long time. His touch felt far away.

Every now and then he would touch my hair with his fingertips. I don't remember the last time Ruben had done that.

I asked him if would he take me upstairs and let me rest in his bed for a while. Without even an answer, he quickly turned his head to Sally and asked her to go get some more cool water. My throat was dry and scratchy and I could hardly swallow, and when I did swallow it felt like a ball of fire.

Ruben made me sip on the cool water even though it was hurting. I asked him had Judith Anne made it back yet. I told him I sure did miss her and little Henry. Judith Anne had told me she was here last month, but I think she's got that all mixed up.

They all lie to me now! One lie after another. Even my sweet Judith Anne. Well, I guess I deserve it. I'm not her beautiful mother anymore. They all look at me as just the woman they keep in the cellar. I know they keep me here so no one will see me.

My God, how long has it been? How long have I been living like this? They're all ashamed of me. I want to die! I bet no one except my family knows I am down here. No one comes to Cedar Grove anymore. I never hear a wagon or a horse coming up the path.

It's totally quiet except for those here on the plantation. I can hear different things, like someone chopping up wood, the cackling of the hens in the chicken house, or maybe a milk cow now and then. I do hear the old rooster every morning. Sometimes hearing him makes me realize that morning has come.

"Lizzy, where is that Judith Anne? She told me she was going to bring little Henry down here today. Where is that girl?"

"She's not here, Miss Abigail! Don't you remember, she had to go back home and take care of something. Remember, she gave you a big hug and said she would be back later," said Lizzy.

"Lizzy, I remember that Miss Bacon had knitted me a shawl. That was the ugliest thing I have ever seen. I would not wear it. In fact, I threw it in the fireplace and watched it burn. The ugly thing went up in smoke. I tell you, Lizzy, I think Judith Anne has become as crazy as all those Bacon women."

Oh my Lord, Miss Abigail, stop talking like that. You know that ain't true. Why would you say something like that? You know Judith Anne is a pretty smart young woman with a good family, and you also know all those Bacons are nice respectable good folks. Now you know that to be true Miss Abigail," said Lizzy.

"I'm not paying any mind to anything you're talking about, Lizzy. You've got where you talk as much as Ruben does."

Lizzy told me I was sick. She told me I don't think like I used to, that all my thoughts were all jumbled up together.

She told me that the things that I say and the things that I do I don't really mean it. She told me I was messed up in my mind. Lizzy said that she thinks all these mixed up thoughts started after little Edmund was born.

I have felt bad for a long time, and now my mother and father don't even come to see me. I asked Lizzy about that and she said that Mother is not well enough to travel like she used to. And she said that it hurts Mother to see me have to live like this.

"Miss Abigail, your mother thinks that Mr. Ruben could have done something else and that he is only thinking of himself. Your mother thinks it is wrong for you to live in the cellar.

Oh Miss Abigail, please, please, I have said too much. You can't say a word to Mr. Ruben about what I said. Mr. Ruben would be so upset with me, and he would not let me stay with you anymore," said Lizzy. "Promise me, Miss Abigail, that you will not say a word. That would get both of us in trouble. You know that, Miss Abigail. I can't believe that I told you what your mother said. I'm so sorry I told you, Miss Abigail," said Lizzy.

You just wait till I see that old goat again. I'll fix him! I hate that Ruben Lewis. All he ever thinks about is himself and what the people of Virginia might think. If the people of Virginia only knew what really goes on here at Cedar Grove they might have a different opinion of things.

That Ruben Lewis has taken me away from my children, my family, and locked me up like a wild animal. I want all of this to end now! This is wrong and this is not right. I don't like it!

They never leave me by myself anymore. If Lizzy has something to do or she has to leave the cellar she will have Chassy or Ettie come watch me. They have taken everything out of my room now. All I have is my bed. They took my two chairs out that day I knocked my windows out. That was a day when Dr. Duke was here. That was also the day that Dr. Duke told Ruben he needed to send me to Williamsburg to that new place.

I'll show all of them. I'll use my stockings and choke myself—that's what I'll do! The bedpost is high enough where I can tie my stocking around the bedpost and tie the other end around my neck. I'll have to pull the stocking hard to make the stocking tight enough to choke me.

I've gotten so weak from not eating, but I think I can do it. I want to do it. I want to die now! They all hate me, so they'll be happy when I'm dead.

XIV
I CAN DO IT

"Lizzy, what are you rattling about now? There you go again, rattling and telling more lies. And another thing, Lizzy: that Martha Elizabeth has a smart mouth on her too. I can tell you she thinks she knows it all. I know she's been sneaking out of the house again after Ruben and I go to bed. She's going over to meet that Thomas Dabney.

"If she gets caught Ruben will not let her leave her room for a week. Martha Elizabeth knows we don't like that kind of thing—sneaking out, going here and there. That's not right, Lizzy. And Martha Elizabeth knows that. People talk about that kind of thing."

"No, no, Miss Abigail, Martha Elizabeth is not doing anything wrong. The Dabney family don't even live around here anymore. They moved over to Westmoreland County, oh, I don't know, going on two to three years now. Mr. Thomas isn't anywhere around here. Remember, Miss Abigail, those are all mixed up thoughts that you have in your mind. We talked about that. We talked about how you get things confused and jumbled up all in your mind," said Lizzy.

"There's nothing mixed up with me! I don't have anything

wrong except being caged up. Turn around, Lizzy. I said turn around! I can't stand to look at you anymore. All you people are the ones that are crazy and mixed up."

"Miss Abigail, I need to go to the kitchen now and also get your clothes. I'll bring another quilt too, cause you'll probably need it. Miss Abigail, now Ettie is going to be right outside your door if you need anything. Just call her and she'll unbolt the door and come on in," said Lizzy.

"How long are you going to be gone, Lizzy?"

"Not long I guess. Why? Is there something else you need, Miss Abigail? What is it, Miss Abigail? What are you wanting?" Lizzy asked.

Lizzy don't know, but I heard her whispering out there with Ettie. I heard her tell Ettie not to open the door no matter what. Now that sounds like Sally! What is Miss Sally doing here? Doesn't she have enough to do? All three of them out there talking. They sound like a bunch of old hens out in the chicken yard.

Sally is out there telling them that I am so thin and pale and getting weaker every day. Now Sally is trying to whisper, but I hear her! Something about what Ruben had told Old Joe, something about me wasting away, and something about my mind and body.

I don't want to hear anything else. They just need to go on. They think I'm crazy, but there is nothing wrong with me. I think in a few days I might feel better and I might get a little stronger. I do feel really weak and I don't really have any strength. But I just don't want to eat anymore. Nothing tastes good.

I had dozed off and did not hear Lizzy come back. I'm so very tired. I just do not have any strength. Maybe if they would bring me some meat and potatoes I would get to feeling better. I can't remember the last time I had any meat or potatoes. All they bring me now is broth and sometimes maybe a few vegetables in there.

Lizzy I need for you to go out to the kitchen and bring me some meat or at least some potatoes. I'm hungry and I want to get stronger. Now go on out there! What are you talking about Miss Abigail. You know there is nothing like that in the kitchen this time of day. What's wrong Miss Abigail? You can not eat any meat anyway. I can bring you some good broth to sip on. They killed two or three old hens this morning real early, so that broth will be real fresh, said Lizzy

Oh for God sakes Lizzy will you get out of my sight. And go on and do whatever you were doing. Just leave me alone. All of you! And you can wipe those tears off your face before you get back. I'm tired of looking at your whiny face. You are a whiny baby Lizzy. You cry more than my babies ever did.

I don't hear any footsteps so I guess Lizzy is gone. And I don't hear Sally either. I don't hear any talking. Maybe they walked off to the kitchen together. Who cares, as long as they're gone. It sure is cold without my stockings and shoes. Now I just have to tie my stockings together and tie one of them tightly to the bedpost. I can't take this any longer. I'm tired of suffering and being away from my family. I have to leave this dungeon today. This has to stop. This has to end.

Lord please give me the strength to finish this. Maybe if I can pull harder I can do it. I'm feeling so sick and it feels as if the inside of my head is going to burst. What is happening, I can taste blood. I feel it on my lips and feel as if I'm choking. Lord please let me die now!

"Who's calling my name? Who is it?"

"It's me, Abby; it's Ruben. Don't try to move or say anything. You are weak and need to rest. We are all here with you and we are not going to leave you. What has happened, Abby? What have you done?" asked Ruben.

What's going on. I can't move. I can't move! Ruben where are you? Lizzy, what's happening? Ruben, for God's sake answer me! Don't you hear me? Answer me!" "Mr. Ruben had to ride to Richmond, but he'll be back in a couple of days. Now lie still so I can bathe your face. You have a little fever, Miss Abigail, so we want to get that out of you. You had a rough night and I guess that's what's brought on the fever," said Lizzy.

"But I'm cold, so I don't have a fever. Is there a fire going? If it is I cannot feel it. I am freezing, Lizzy! Will you have Uncle Pete to tell one of the boys to bring in some more wood? Then tell them to get the fire going real good to warm up this room.

"I sure do love Sally. Do you know, Lizzy, that Sally helps me with my babies? Lizzy, where are my girls? Where have those girls disappeared to? And my little Edmund is growing so much. He is almost a young man now. Where is that boy, Lizzy!"

"Miss Abigail, he's upstairs napping. You know he likes to nap this time of day. And the girls are doing their schooling," said Lizzy.

"Napping! What are you talking about, Lizzy? That boy is about grown; he does not need to be napping. Ruben will not like that. He'll make that boy get out and do some work. Ruben does not believe in children sitting around. He believes they should be doing something and so do I. Go tell Miss Sally to get that boy up. Sally, are you here?" "Yes, I'm here, Miss Abigail. I'll go upstairs right now and tell Edmund he needs to go outside and do some work. I would not want Mr. Ruben to find out Edmund is napping," said Sally.

"Miss Sally, I've been meaning to ask you, is that old Master Campbell still messing with your sweet Lucy? Cause if he is Ruben will take care of him too. You just let Ruben know now. Ruben don't like that kind of thing.

"What's wrong, Sally? Why are you crying? Did Mother say something to hurt your feelings again?"

"No, no, Miss Abigail, your mother did not do anything to me. Your mother has always been good to me and treated me real nice. You know, Miss Abigail, I've been thinking lately about when you were a little girl. You were always running around Mount Laurel, getting into all kind of mischief. You would have your mother and father all worried. Miss Abigail, your mother always wanted all you children to grow up and be good respectable folks. And all of y'all have done that. Your mother is very proud of you," said Sally.

"Lizzy, did you show Miss Sally the beautiful wildflowers that Uncle Pete brought me this morning? He knows the blue ones are my favorite. Uncle Pete is very good to me. He helps me with just about anything I need. We haven't been on a walk in the woods lately. I'll have to tell Uncle Pete that we need to do that soon."

XV
MY SWEET ABBY

"Why is Ruben not here! He can't be talking to Uncle Pete this long. Ruben does like to talk, but never mind. And why in God's name was old lady Carr here yesterday?. She has been fussing at me again. I tell you Lizzy I don't trust that old woman. I think she's up to no good.

She wants to hurt me, Lizzy! She did have something behind her back. She was trying to hide it, but I could see her. She was sneaking around like a rat. I'm afraid of her Lizzy."

"No, don't you be afraid, Miss Abigail. Nobody is going to hurt you. Sally and I are here with you. Now you stop that crying, Miss Abigail; you don't want your fever to come back. You know when you get real upset that fever comes, and Sally wants to sit with you for a while. Sally stays so busy tending to the children she doesn't get to come to the cellar like she wants to," said Lizzy.

"Oh my God, here we go again. It's that James Randolph. He and Ruben will be talking all night. Ruben wants me to wear that peach silk dress tonight when he will be socializing with those men from Richmond. I tell you, Lizzy, I don't want to talk and be up half the night with those old men. And there will be all that drinking too; there always is. And the smoke fills my whole house. I don't know why Ruben has all those men here so much. I am so tired of all those men stopping by here. It's been that way ever since we moved to Cedar Grove."

"You don't have to talk to them, Miss Abigail. Those men folks are friends of Mr. Ruben's. They got stuff to talk about I guess. You said they talk a lot about Virginia, so maybe that's why they're here so much. Let's don't talk about them anymore. Let's talk about you, Miss Abigail," said Lizzy. "Do you want another sip of water? You need to drink more water. And before long I'm going to bring you some hot broth again to warm your stomach. You got to keep something on your stomach, Miss Abigail. You got where you don't eat anything and you know that," said Lizzy.

"What is that noise, Lizzy? It's a peck-peck noise. What is that? Is that someone trying to break in? I don't like that noise, Lizzy. That scares me. Don't let them hurt us! Lizzy, I think you need to run and try to find Ruben or Old Joe before they get in here and hurt us."

"There's no one out there, Miss Abigail. I promise you that. No one is here and no one is going to hurt us. Do you know what that is, Miss Abigail? That is sleet. It has started sleeting and that pecking noise is cause the wind is blowing it against your windows. Listen, Miss Abigail. Do you hear that? I promise you that's all that is," said Lizzy.

"Lizzy, did I tell you that Madison likes to play in the snow with no gloves on? Then I have to rub his little hands together in front of the fire to warm him up. Then he cries cause his

MY SWEET ABBY

little hands are stinging from the cold. Ruben tells me that I treat him like a baby. He tells me, 'That boy is almost seven years old now, so don't be treating him like he is two.' Men just don't understand children and how to take care of them. But I did good with my children. I think I did anyway. My mother likes for the children to come sometimes and stay with her. I think they like that too. Sarah and Edmund love the ride to Mount Laurel. It's tiring for them, but they say they have fun with Benson. Ruben usually has Benson to take them there.

"I think tomorrow I'll make Catherine Louise a new dress. I think I'll make her a lavender one. That will go so pretty with her blonde curls, and the color lavender is so pretty in the spring. Buttercup yellow and lavender let you know spring is here.

"Sally, I want to sleep. Will you help me out of bed so I can lie in front of my fireplace? I'm so cold. I've got to get warm. I'm shaking I'm so cold. Have those boys brought us more wood? I think we need some. And Ruben and Uncle Pete both are always telling them to make sure we have enough wood down here in the cellar."

"Miss Abigail, I don't think this is a good idea. You're not very strong and I don't think you need to get out of the bed. You just need to lie there and try to get some sleep. We can talk till you dose off to sleep. We always like talking together, don't we?" said Sally.

"Wait a minute, wait a minute! What's going on! Who in God's name tied my hands and feet to the bed? Who was it! I know who it was. I bet it was that old Dr. Duke. Lizzy, you

☙ 71 ❧

promised me that I would not have to see that old goat again. You promised me!"

"Now come on, Miss Abigail, stop talking mess about Dr. Duke. Dr. Duke has not been here. I promise you he has not been here! Now you're getting yourself all upset for no reason. It's not good for you to get upset, you know that. Now calm down, Miss Abigail. Calm down, please. Dr. Duke knows you're sick in your mind. He knows you get all your thoughts jumbled up. He knows that. And he was just here to try to help you. Dr. Duke cares about you. He was trying to help you with your thoughts and feelings," said Lizzy.

"If that old man puts his hands on me again I'll bite him till he bleeds out! And he's the one that wanted to send me away. I heard him and Ruben talking that day. They don't know that I heard them, but I did. He wanted to send me somewhere over in Williamsburg. I could not hear everything, but I heard enough.

"Lizzy, I have to wet. Do you hear me, woman? I have to wet. My God, woman, listen to what I'm telling you. All you people are crazy. Y'all never want to listen to me and y'all never have. You never have wanted to know how I feel.

And Lizzy you can untie me right this minute. I want out of this bed. Listen to me people, I want out of this bed. And Sally what are you crying about again."

"Miss Abigail, Mr. Ruben told all of us not to untie you. He said you were too weak and he did not want you to fall," said Sally.

"Why does everybody like to hurt me? I didn't do anything

to them. Like that Ruben—he's off who knows where prob-ably bedding up with some woman. He's probably with that Eleanor Fontaine. That woman is ugly and has hips on her like a worn out old sow. How could any man be with that ugly woman?"

"Lord, Miss Abigail, you have said enough! Child, what has happened to you? I cannot believe what's coming out of your mouth. I'm sure you don't know what you're saying, and what you're saying is just plain silly talk. Mr. Ruben loves you and would not do that kind of thing. That's just devil talk coming out of your mouth, Miss Abigail. That's nothing but pure devil talk! Now you lie still and don't be squirming all around. When you squirm around like that it rubs on your wrist and ankles," said Lizzy.

I began to get real weak and sleepy again. I could barely hear Sally and Lizzy. They were talking softly on the other side of my room. Then I heard someone unbolt my door, but I never heard them speak. I was so tired I could not open my eyes.

"Sally, I don't think I can take anymore of this. What is going to happen to Miss Abigail and those children upstairs? It hurts me and brings me tears to see Miss Abigail suffer like she does. She's been suffering for a long time now. Sally, I've never seen anyone with a mind like Miss Abigail has now," said Lizzy.

"Lizzy, I don't know what to say. Miss Abigail is so differ-ent now. It seems like it came in her mind after little Edmund was born. It just came over her like a spell. She don't even look right, Lizzy. She don't even look like the same woman," said

Sally.

"Sally, what does Mr. Ruben do all these times he is gone? Lord, I might not should say this, but I think that man needs to be here more with Miss Abigail. I guess Mr. Ruben is taking care of some kind of business that we don't know nothing about. Sally, I need to get out of this cellar for a few minutes," said Lizzy.

"Miss Sally, where did Lizzy go? I don't hear her stirring around. Did I tell you, Miss Sally, that Isabel is coming tomorrow to see me? I've missed her so much. Mother always lets Isabel and I stay up half the night talking. Mother said that we would do it anyway. Father gets upset sometimes, so we go to the parlor far away from Father."

XVI
CHILDREN'S VISIT

"Mr. Ruben, I'm glad you're here cause Miss Abigail is not doing good at all. She's so bony now and her talking doesn't make any sense. She talks about things that ain't happening, and she thinks strange things too, Mr. Ruben. She thinks people are here when they are not.

"She just ain't the same person, Mr. Ruben. Miss Abigail is so messed up in her mind, and well, it's just scary, Mr. Ruben. It's just plain scary for all of us! I'm not afraid of Miss Abigail, but some of the other slaves are. They just don't know what she may do. They're scared for her and they're scared for them," said Lizzy.

"I know, Lizzy. I don't think Abby has tried for weeks now, and she doesn't even look like my Abby anymore. And her mind, well, I don't know what to say about that. Her mind is gone, Lizzy. I don't know, Lizzy, maybe I should have taken Abby to Williamsburg. Dr. Duke did suggest that. But I wanted to keep Abby here with us," said Ruben.

"Come with me, Mr. Ruben; let me show you something. Look how bony she's gotten. And you know, Mr. Ruben, that I've always tried to make her eat and I always tried to do what was right for her. But I tell you, her being taken away from her children and away from you has made things worse," said Lizzy.

"And her temper, Lizzy, oh my gosh. I'm telling you, Lizzy, Abby would go into rages over nothing, just little things. The children seem to get on her nerves and upset her very much. All of Abby's softness and tenderness seemed to disappear after Edmund was born. And Abby used to love to entertain. Oh, she's always had one or two things to say about me talking too much, but it was all in a joking way. Sometimes after everyone had left Abby would ask me if was I talked out. Then we would both laugh and then we would go on our way," said Ruben. "But then it got to a point where she would go into complete rages over nothing. I mean nothing, Lizzy. Just for no reason her complete body would change into someone else. I hadn't seen that look or those actions on Abby before.

"The look on her face, the look in her eyes, and everything else changed. I didn't know what else to do but to put her in the cellar. With her outburst and rages, I do not know what else I could have done Lizzy. Lizzy, you don't know how people talk outside of this plantation. It's different out there, Lizzy, not like it is here at Cedar Grove. People can say some cruel things, things they really don't know anything about. And bad talking is not good! Not at all," said Ruben.

"What do you mean 'bad talking,' Mr. Ruben? Mr. Ruben, maybe you should be thinking more about Miss Abigail than bad talking. I don't know anything about what you do and your business, Mr. Ruben, but Miss Abigail needs you and those babies of hers. Maybe I'm just a stupid old woman, but I am the one that's been down here in this cellar with Miss Abigail for all this time. I'm the one that has listened to her cry and beg me to let her out. I've watched her look out her windows at the children playing in the back and maybe in some way she knew she could never be with them again.

"And poor Miss Abigail doesn't even know much about her last baby like a mother should. It breaks my heart to know that Miss Abigail will die in the cellar, and she will die not knowing why she was put down here," said Lizzy.

"Lizzy, I didn't mean to hurt your feelings, but you don't understand how it is out there. Things are different. I can't explain it—just different. I'm sorry I made you cry, Lizzy. I am very sorry! I know it's been very hard on you having to live like this and care for Abby. Come on, Lizzy, please don't cry. I know there have been times that you have not been able to see your boys like you wanted to, and I am sorry for that too. Sally, you have not said anything all this time we've been talking. Is there anything you want to say? What do you think about Abby?" Ruben asked.

"Well, Mr. Ruben, I agree with Lizzy. Miss Abigail is not doing good at all. Her mind is all gone. Mr. Ruben, let's untie Miss Abigail so she will be more comfortable. Let's try that for a while and see what happens. I don't think we have to tie her to the bed any longer. I think she's too weak, so she will not try to get out of bed," said Sally.

"Sally, this afternoon you go upstairs and tell the children that we're going to visit their mother later today. I know it's been hard on the children to see their mother in this condition, but I think they need to visit her today. Do you have any idea where Madison is?" asked Ruben.

"Don't rightly know, sir. He might be over at Miss Jane's. Hard to really tell where he goes these days. But Benson was saying the other day that Madison has been spending almost part of every day with Jane. I will walk out with you, Mr. Ruben," said Sally.

"Sally, have you ever known a woman to get bad off in her mind like Abby You know what I mean: like they don't know what they're doing most of the time, and they are confused and frustrated about different things, and all their thoughts go into a rage for no reason," asked Ruben.

"Well sir, not but one or two I guess. And it was also after birthing. Not right after, but a few weeks or maybe a few months. I don't remember. Oh, Mr. Ruben, those women never got their minds to work again like they should. One of them did a horrible thing—one woman over at Live Oaks down from Sweet Pine kept her baby in a washtub till he drowned. That woman never left her room again. No one could believe she had killed her own baby. They say she was so sweet and kind and was a loving woman until that happened. They said everybody was afraid of her after that. Talk was that she would always knock out her windows when she got mad. They said at the end she just had a quilt hung over her window.

Some say she jumped out of the window one night, but I don't know if that's true or not. I really don't know what ever happened to her. Oh, Mr. Ruben, we need all the strength the Lord will give us. We will make it, Mr. Ruben; somehow we will. I'm going on in the house now and tend to the children," said Sally.

"I've got some thinking to do, Sally, so it will be a while before I want you to bring the children down to the cellar. I will let you know when I am ready. And if you hear or see Madison please come tell me," said Ruben.

"Are you here, Ruben? Do I hear you? Please answer me, Ruben. I want you to stay down here with me for a while. It's been a long time since you spent the night here. Please spend the night with me tonight!"

"Oh, Miss Abigail, Mr. Ruben has gone back upstairs. He was down here with you for quite a while. He sat with you and talked with you. He's got some things to do right now but he said he would be back later to see you, and he's going to bring the children down this afternoon to see you. That will be nice because it's been a while since you've seen your children. They're going to be happy when they see you again," said Lizzy.

"Children! Who said anything about children? I don't want those children down here. They will be making so much noise and will not do what I tell them to do, and that Ruben never makes them behave. He will let them do whatever they want, just like he always does. I don't understand why Ruben does that to me. He knows that upsets me so much to have all the children around. They make me confused. They make me where I don't know what I'm doing.

"Hey, Lizzy, I think I hear a wagon coming down the path. Yeah, I do, I bet that is Isabel. She did come back as she promised. We will have so much fun tonight. We can stay up all night again. Father will be upset like he always is, but Mother does not care.

"Go out there, Lizzy, and tell Old Joe to meet Isabel—or maybe Uncle Pete can do it if he is not too busy. He has not seen Isabel in a long time either, so he will like that. And I hope to God that Isabel did not bring that loud husband of hers, or those rowdy children. I tell you, Lizzy, I don't see how Isabel stands all that noise. She's got some bad children, but maybe she left them with her mother."

"Martha Elizabeth, go find Catherine Louise, Sarah, and Edmund. We are going down to the cellar this afternoon to visit with your mother. Your mother is very weak and I think today is the day that we need to go down there as a family," said Ruben.

"Oh Father, Catherine Louise will not go to the cellar anymore. She was down there a few weeks ago and Mother looked so bad that she told me she would never go back down there. She said that Mother was very thin and very pale and did not make any sense when she would talk. And I believe Sarah is afraid to go down there too," said Martha Elizabeth.

"It will be hard on us to go down to the cellar as a family, but it is something we have to do. Your mother might not recognize some of us and she probably will not make a lot of sense if she does talk, but we have to do this for her and for us. She is your mother and she loved you children very, very much. I am so very sorry that she has not been with you children for the last few years. I really did do what I thought was best for Abby and for you children. It breaks my heart to know that Abby was taken away from me and you children," said Ruben. "And as to why the Lord has chosen to take my Abby away from me and away from you children, I do not know. I have asked myself that for years now, but there has never been an answer. I know that your mother is tired and weak, but we need to see her as a family together again, and I think it has to be today. I don't think we can wait any longer. Do you understand what I mean?" asked Ruben.

XVII
OFF TO RICHMOND

"Old Joe, I'm going to have to ride to Richmond tomorrow. Can you have my horse and things ready at dawn? I've got a very long day ahead of me, so I want to get a real early start," said Ruben.

"Are you sure you want to go with the sky looking like it does? You know it sure looks like snow, and you know how it is around here when it does snow. It makes a lot of trouble for everyone, and you wouldn't want to get caught up in all that, Mr. Ruben. Maybe in a day or so it will clear up. What do you think, Mr. Ruben?" asked Old Joe.

"The only thing is that I have to be gone three or four days, so the sooner I leave the sooner I can get back here. And with Abby being in the shape she is in I want to go and get back as quickly as I can," said Ruben.

"Oh I do understand, Mr. Ruben, yes sir, I sure do. What is most important is Miss Abigail. What can I do to help Miss Abigail while you are gone? Cause you know all of us around here want to do whatever we can to help you and Miss Abigail. We all know Miss Abigail is not right in her mind. We know she's changed. Betsy was saying the other day that she has not been to the cellar in many, many weeks. And I don't think Larkin says much of anything about Miss Abigail. I think they want to remember Miss Abigail as she used to be," said Old Joe.

"You know I think I'll have a brandy or two and read some before retiring. I have a full day tomorrow, so I need some rest for sure. I hate to leave Abby in this condition. That woman has endured so much pain in the past few years. And also, Old Joe, when Madison gets back will you tell him to please join me for a brandy? Ruben asked.

"Hello, Madison, I'm glad you're back. Please join me in a brandy. Madison, I need for you to stay close around here for the next few days, at least till I get back from Richmond. You know how weak your mother is so one of us has to be here at all times. We both cannot be gone, not at this point! I sure do not want to leave Abby, but I do not have a choice," said Ruben.

"I will be here, Father. In fact, I told Jane tonight that I could not come back to Locust Grove for a while because Mother is not doing well at all, and of course she understood. Father, I would like to sit with Mother for a while and let Lizzy get out of the cellar and rest for a couple of hours. It breaks my heart to see Mother the way she is. She is just skin and bones. Lizzy tells me that Mother will not eat anything. She has tried and tried to get Mother to eat. And now, Mother will not even drink," said Madison.

XVIII
MADISON'S FEAR

"I'm so glad you are here, Mr. Madison. We have had such a bad day. It seems to get worse hour after hour. Chassy was down here earlier to help me, but I think she is now afraid of Miss Abigail, so she didn't stay long. Sally was down here too, but she had to get back upstairs and tend to the children. This is so hard on Sally. You know, Mr. Madison, Sally has been with your mother for many years. Miss Abigail was just a little girl when Sally came to Mount Laurel. Sally mostly stayed in the main house tending to Miss Abigail, her sisters, and her mother. Sally loved all of them, and I think they loved Sally too," said Lizzy.

"And there has been nothing on Miss Abigail's stomach for days—not even anything to drink. I've tried and tried, but she just won't swallow anything. She won't let anything go down. She's lost so much weight. When Sally and I tried to feed her she would turn her head when the spoon would touch her lips, and sometimes it would just run down her chin. Sally would cry when Miss Abigail would do that. I think your mother has given up, Mr. Madison," said Lizzy.

"Lizzy, why don't you get out of the cellar for a while? I will sit with Mother. We will be fine, I promise. Now, Lizzy, you bundle up good because it's awful cold out there, and the wind has picked up straight out of the north. Can't have you sick, Lizzy. I hate that Father has to go to Richmond tomorrow. But I guess he knows what is best, said Madison.

"Can you hear me, Mother? I love you, Mother. I wish you would eat something to gain your strength back. Sally and Lizzy are here to help you and to get you whatever you need or want. Mother, Jane and I are going to marry in the spring. She will make a good wife and I do love her. I'm looking into buying the old Nathaniel Ball place. Since Mr. Ball's death his wife has gotten sick. Joseph Ball said he's going to have his mother live at his place and sell Belvedere.

"I want to talk to Father about it when he returns from Richmond. Now, Mother, you have to start eating again so Chassy can make you a new dress for the wedding. And Ettie can tie your hair up with a pretty silk ribbon. You will look so pretty, Mother, in your new dress.

"Oh, Mother, please don't give up! You have to try for all of us, but mostly for yourself. We don't want to lose you, Mother. I know it's terrible down here, and I know that you and Lizzy have been through a lot of pain having to live in the cellar, but please try, Mother," said Madison.

"You are right, Mr. Madison; it's a terrible wind out there. And it is straight out of the north. I brought me back some hot tea hoping that might warm me up. Sally said she's going to pack Mr. Ruben some good food in case he is gone longer than he usually is. We are all worried that Mr. Ruben is riding off when the sky looks so bad.

Mr. Madison while you are here I think I'll lay some quilts in front of the fireplace for Miss Abigail to lie on. It's been a while since she lay in front of the fire. She sure does like to do that. I think these three quilts will be soft enough for her. Now let's just try to gently pick up your mother so we can lay her right in front of the fire. Please be careful with her, Mr. Madison, because she has sores on her backside and arms. I'll have to put some more stuff on her," said Lizzy.

"Oh, Lizzy, look at Mother. She is so frail and delicate. I'm so afraid I'm going to hurt her. I want to be so gentle with her. I don't even know if Mother can hear me. I was talking to her about Jane and I. I told Mother that we are to marry in the Spring. And we would have Chassy make her a new dress, said Madison.

Oh, Mr. Madison, I don't believe Miss Abigail can hear you. I hope she did, but I don't know. And Miss Abigail might not know who you are either. You know, Mr. Madison, that your mother's mind is gone, and that she hasn't had thoughts or feelings in the right way for a very long time. I think she knew many times how confused she was, and I think she knew how jumbled up everything was in her mind," said Lizzy.

I'm so afraid Lizzy. My poor Mother.

"Mr. Ruben, Mr. Ruben, wake up, sir. It's almost dawn and Sally has got your coffee boiling, and your food is almost ready too. I don't know about this weather, Mr. Ruben. It sure don't look right to me. No sir, it sure don't. I don't know about all of this. I'm so scared it's not going to be good riding weather," said Old Joe.

"Oh my God, I cannot believe I overslept. I guess I was more tired than I thought I was. I am sorry, Old Joe. Would you please tell Sally that I'll be right there? Yeah, it does look like it's going to be a cold day and I'm sure dreading leaving. Just let me get my boots on and I'll be right there," said Ruben.

"Mr. Ruben, you've got a nose like a fox. I can never surprise you when it comes to my fried pork and biscuits, and I've got some of that good gravy that you like. Now you sip on this hot coffee till I get your plate ready," said Sally.

"Sally, it tickles me to think back when Abby and I first got married. I do believe if it had not been for your good cooking that all of us would have starved to death. Cause let's face it, Sally, you and I both know Abby was not the best cook. She tried and and tried. But that never worked. Sometimes she would tell me how she had been out to the kitchen with y'all trying to learn some stuff," said Ruben.

"Mr. Ruben, sir, please don't cry. If you get yourself all worked up it will just make your trip harder to do, and I know you want to take care of your business and get on back here to Miss Abigail. Now, sir, you need to go on and finish your food so you can get on the road. I'm almost finished packing your food to take with you. I packed it last night but thought of a few more things that I should put in there," said Sally.

"Sally, is that you?" asked Lizzy.

"Yeah, I just wanted to tell you that Mr. Ruben is gone. He kind of got a late start, but I made sure he had some extra food before he left. Mr. Ruben sure hated to leave this morning.

His eyes filled with water when he got to talking about Miss Abigail. He was talking about Miss Abigail's cooking when they first got married. He has always loved Miss Abigail," said Sally

"Miss Abigail, do you want to go back to your bed? Miss Abigail? Well, that's all right I reckon. You can lie there in front of the fire as long as you are comfortable. I hope you are warm enough, Miss Abigail. It is so cold in here. We've got a good fire going and plenty of wood to last us, but it is still cold. And it is so damp down here, and seems to get worse each winter," said Lizzy

"Lizzy, why don't you let me stay here a while and you go on and fix you a plate. Ettie is still in the kitchen and there is some pork and biscuits left over. I know you haven't eaten anything yourself in a few days—at least not much of anything. And while you're out there, why don't you stop by and see Betsy and Larkin? They are always asking about you and Miss Abigail. And what about Belle? It would be nice if you stopped by to see her and to see how she is doing," said Sally.

"I hate to leave her, Sally. She has given up. She only said two or three words yesterday and then last night she spit up green and yellow mess. But she hasn't had anything on her stomach for days now," said Lizzy.

"Good morning, Lizzy! You come on in here and sit down and eat you something. We got plenty left over. Sally said Mr. Ruben ate good before he left and the children have eaten too. You know those children just pick at their food, especially Sarah and Edmund. But with things the way they are around here I don't guess nobody feels much like eating," said Ettie.

"I tell you, Ettie, Miss Abigail spit up all night. I'm so worried about her. Mr. Ruben asked me had I ever heard of a woman whose mind had got like Miss Abigail's after birthing. Mr. Ruben said that he had never heard of a woman's mind getting like that.

"I don't know if Mr. Ruben knows this or not, but one time Miss Abigail grabbed Sarah's little arm and twisted it. She did not mean to hurt Sarah, but it did happen. She just wanted her to stop running in and out of the house. When that happened Miss Abigail started screaming and crying and ran outside the house and sat under that big sugar maple out back.

"Miss Abigail cried for days after that. She felt so bad that she had hurt little Sarah's arm. After a while I don't think Miss Abigail remembered half of the things she had done when she would go into a rage. She would kind of change, just do and say things I had never heard or seen her do before. She was like somebody I did not know.

"I don't know why this happened to such a sweet girl. She has always been so sweet and kind to everybody. And Sally said she was a loving child too. Even at all their social gatherings here at Cedar Grove she would enjoy talking and being around everyone. She would laugh and talk and just have a good time when Mr. Ruben would have folks over.

"And she would always find time to help someone when they needed it. I just do not understand all of this, Ettie. But I do know that all of this started to happen after birthing Edmund—maybe not at first, but not long after.

"I'm sorry, Ettie, I did not mean to upset you more. I will

just finish up my food and then maybe I can rest some. I am so tired. Sally is with Miss Abigail now, so I know she will be taken care of. Ettie, this food is so good. I was so hungry. I think after I rest I will walk over to see Benson and Belle. I haven't seen them for going on two weeks or so. Belle sure is getting big with that baby. And Benson is so crazy about that girl and always has been. They get along pretty good I guess," said Lizzy.

"Old Joe, what in Gods name is wrong with you! Don't come busting in here like a scalded dog. Have you lost all your senses? What's wrong?" asked Lizzy.

"Lizzy, come quick! It's Miss Abigail. She is coughing up chunks of blood and she's real hot with fever too. Sally told me to run and get you," said Old Joe.

"I'm here, Miss Abigail. I'm not gonna leave you anymore. Everything is going to be okay. Let me see if I can get that out of your throat. You will be okay, Miss Abigail; I promise you that," said Lizzy. "Old Joe, help me here. I need to turn Miss Abigail's head to one side over the pot. I've got to get this blood out of her throat because she's choking on the blood. I'm not going to hurt you, Miss Abigail; you know that. I just want to help you breathe better. I won't hurt you. That's good, Miss Abigail! Let's get all that old blood out of you.

"Old Joe, you go and empty this pot and bring me two more quilts from upstairs. Before you go, let's turn her on her side in case there is more blood. And also bring me some more cool water and another cloth. My God, Miss Abigail is burning up hot again. This fever has to come out of her. Well, hurry up,

Old Joe; this child is burning up," said Lizzy.

"Do you want to try to move Miss Abigail back to her bed? What do you think, Lizzy? Should we move her or what? Or do you think it's best to leave her where she is in front of the fire?" asked Sally.

"I'm not going to leave you, Miss Abigail. I've got you. Let me wrap this quilt a little tighter around you, cause I know you're cold. Hold on, Miss Abigail, and don't give up! You hold on and get better for your babies upstairs. They need you, Miss Abigail, and you need them. Don't give up, please!

"You know how you would always tell me that you could hear their little footsteps above you when they were walking in the eating room? Remember how we talked about how loud Sarah and Edmund were? We could always hear so much down here in the cellar. We could hear so much of what was going on upstairs.

"And you know that Mr. Madison and Miss Jane are getting married soon, so we have to get you all pretty again. Mr. Madison wants Chassy to make you a new dress, and maybe next time Mr. Ruben goes to Richmond or Williamsburg he can pick you up some silk ribbon for your hair. I want to brush your hair and tie it back with a ribbon like I used to do for you. Won't that be nice, Miss Abigail," asked Lizzy.

"I'm so afraid, Lizzy. Miss Abigail looks so bad. I can't do this! I can't stand to see Miss Abigail looking like this. What are we going to do, Lizzy? I can't believe she's so tiny and pale," said Sally.

"Sally, for God's sake would you please be quiet! I know

what Miss Abigail looks like. And for God's sake, where is the water and cloth I asked Old Joe to go get! Where is that man! Where is he! Sally, wipe her mouth, please. That blood keeps coming out, and I don't know where it's coming from—her stomach, I guess. Let's keep bathing her face and arms, cause this fever is bad. My God, where is the fresh water?" asked Lizzy.

"Sally you need to go get Mr. Madison and tell him he needs to come to the cellar right now. Whatever he's doing he needs to stop and come down here with his mother. Miss Abigail is very bad off. I cannot believe Mr. Ruben is not here! That man needs to be here with Miss Abigail. And tell Mr. Madison do not say a word to the children. And Sally, bring me two more shifts for Miss Abigail when you come back. This one is . . . well . . . just bring me two more. She has soiled this one real bad," said Lizzy.

"Mother, Mother, what's happening? I love you, Mother! I love you! Lizzy, what is wrong with Mother? Why does she look like this? What's going on? I'm so afraid, Lizzy."

"Catherine Louise, wait a minute! Don't come down here. I need for you to go back upstairs and don't say anything to the other children. I need for you to check on Sarah and Edmund, because Sally will be down here for a while and I don't know where Martha Elizabeth is," said Madison.

"Sally, I'm ready for her clean shift now. Do you think somebody needs to ride to Richmond to fetch Mr. Ruben? I'll tell you, Sally, Miss Abigail is barely hanging on, and I don't know how long it will be now. I just don't know, Sally. I'm so afraid and I would never forgive myself if Mr. Ruben was not here. I don't know anything else to do," said Lizzy.

"Yes, Lizzy, I think Mr. Ruben needs to be here. I know you have done everything that could have been done to help Miss Abigail. I think the Lord is getting ready for her. I know he is. This child cannot stand any more of this cellar. Look at her, Lizzy. She's all curled up like a baby. And she is so tiny," said Sally.

"Sally, I have tried so hard to make her eat and drink, and you have too. I think Miss Abigail felt like there was no reason for her to go on. I think she had enough left in her mind to know she would never be able to live upstairs again, and I think she knew Mr. Ruben would never hear of it.

"I'm sure she felt like she could not take anymore months or years down here in the cellar. I do believe somehow in Miss Abigail's mind she knew things would never get better after Mr. Ruben put us down here. I don't know how she knew, but I think she did. And, Sally, I have to tell you: I don't think Mr. Ruben did Miss Abigail really right.

He put us down here in a place that does not even have a stone floor—nothing, Sally, but dirt. It's been cold on us down here. Sure, we've always had a good fire when we needed one, but it was always damp. I'm sorry, Sally, but that's just the way I feel. Maybe Mr. Ruben did not have a choice; I don't know. All I know is Miss Abigail needed Mr. Ruben and those children," said Lizzy.

"Oh my Lord, Lizzy, blood is coming out of her mouth again. Hurry, let's turn her over before she chokes. It's been going off and on all day. Lizzy, I think we have to send some-body to Richmond now. I don't think we can wait any longer. Somebody's got to go find Mr. Ruben," said Sally.

"Sally, go tell Old Joe to tell Benson to ride and get Mr. Ruben. And go tell Mr. Madison what has to be done. Sally, you go and stay with the children and I'll be here with Miss Abigail," said Lizzy.

"Mr. Madison, Mr. Madison, come quickly. Your father needs to be here. Miss Abigail has gotten worse and I just don't know, Mr. Madison. Lizzy said Benson should ride to Richmond and try to find Mr. Ruben," said Sally.

"Benson, Mother is very bad off, so I need for you to ride to Richmond and find Father. Here is a good horse and some supplies for you. I hate to see you ride out in all of this, but it's Mother, Benson, and Father needs to be here at Cedar Grove," said Madison.

"Oh that's all right Mr. Madison. I don't mind. Just let me put on more clothes and some more boots and I'll be right back. I don't mind doing whatever it takes for Miss Abigail. And don't you worry, Mr. Madison—I'll find Mr. Ruben," said Benson.

XIX
HER LIBERTY

"I want to hug Mother, Lizzy. Is that okay? Can she feel my touch? Does she know I'm here? What's happening, Lizzy?" asked Madison.

"Your mother's hands are so cold. One minute she has fever and the next her skin is cold, and she has been spitting up blood all day. I sure hope Benson finds your father in time. Mr. Ruben sure needs to be here. I'm sorry, Mr. Madison, but I don't think Mr. Ruben should have left with Miss Abigail being like this," said Lizzy.

"Lizzy, I think in a few minutes I need to go upstairs and sit with the children while they eat. I don't want Sarah or Edmund to know what's really going on, but I do want to tell them that Father is coming home early. I won't be able to eat anything, but I still think I need to sit at the table with the children. Can I bring you back anything, Lizzy?" asked Madison.

"No, no, sir, I could not eat anything. I'm just going to stay here with Miss Abigail and pray Benson gets to Richmond safe. He's a strong boy, so I know he will be fine. But if you would, tell Sally I need her to come to the cellar with me for a while," said Lizzy.

"Lizzy, what can I do to help? Mr. Madison said you need-ed me. Look at her just lying there as if there's no life left in her at all. That child is just worn out. Her mind has been gone for a while and now there's not much left of her little body. Lizzy, I'm going to have to leave the cellar for a few minutes or so, cause I'm sick on my stomach," said Sally.

"Mr. Ruben, Mr. Ruben, I'm sorry, but you have to get back to Cedar Grove as fast as you can. Miss Abigail is not do-ing good at all. They say she's real, real weak, and she has been spitting up blood," said Benson.

Mr. Ruben got his horse and left Richmond as quick as he could. He was trying to beat time, and time was not something that Mr. Ruben had. As he was leaving Richmond, he thought, I'll never make it. Not in this weather. He only stopped at the Hanover Tavern to let Miss Abigail's mother and father know that his Abby was worse off.

Mr. Ruben quickly changed horses at the tavern and inn's stables and continued to ride to Cedar Grove. So many emotions ran through Mr. Ruben's body as he made his way through the rain and sleet back to his Abby. He knew she could not hold on much longer.

As the rain pounded his clothes he could only think of the years that he and Miss Abigail had before she got sick. Miss Abigail was only fifteen when they met. Miss Abigail was talk-ing to Thomas Southall out on the porch at Mount Laurel. Her father was having a social gathering as he did so often before moving to the Hanover Inn.

Thomas seemed to have a way with beautiful young ladies.

He spoke well and was handsome. He was also educated and would be attending William and Mary. All the young ladies enjoyed talking to him, but when Miss Abigail turned around there was Mr. Ruben. She had seen Mr. Ruben before, but that had been a year back. She had seen him at another social gathering her grandfather was having.

Miss Abigail had once told me she thought Mr. Ruben was a little too rustic for her. His clothing did not seem to be one of a true Virginia gentleman. She said that night she saw Mr. Ruben at Mount Laurel that she didn't pay too much attention to what he was wearing. She said she quickly excused herself from Mr. Southall and began talking to Mr. Ruben.

I guess it was love right away. After that night Mr. Ruben made a number of trips out to Mount Laurel. At first, Miss Abigail's older sister was hoping Mr. Ruben was there to see her, but she quickly realized it was Miss Abigail that he was interested in. Mr. Ruben and Miss Abigail were married later that year at Mount Laurel.

As Mr. Ruben continued riding toward Cedar Grove, the wind and the rain continued and so did the sleet, and it seemed to get colder with each mile he rode. There had been a snowfall earlier that month and all the snow had melted, but now there was a good chance of another snowfall. As Mr. Ruben rode as hard as he could the sleet began to stick to his clothes. He was praying all the way to Cedar Grove.

I could hear the ice pecking on Miss Abigail's window . What a sad and lonely sound it made each time the ice hit the window. I kept adding good old hickory logs to the fire in hopes that somehow it would make Miss Abigail feel better. But I guess I really knew it was me that needed to feel better, cause there was no hope for Miss Abigail. I don't think she ever knew how close the end was.

She was so weak and wasn't even moving. She just lay there on her quilts in front of the fire like she had done so many times in the past three years. As I sat there beside her in front of the fire I softly brushed her long, beautiful black hair and softly sang to her, hoping she might call my name.

But she just lay there like a child, lying on her side, staring into the fire with no emotions at all. She was looking all at peace. Every now and then she would slowly try to reach out for my other hand, which was resting on her once-beautiful face. Miss Abigail had always been a beautiful woman, with her long black hair, her beautiful black eyes, and her rosy cheeks. Even her sweet lips had a rosy color to them. They used to say Abigail Lewis was the most beautiful woman between here and Richmond.

Her body had now become so bony and thin, and in the past few weeks all she would do is spit everything up, even when there was nothing there. Her body had now become sick, sick like her mind had been for three years. My sweet Miss Abigail had sores on her back and arms from not moving much at all. She just gave up, I'm sure.

As she lay in front of her fire with just her cotton shift around her little thin body I took her quilts and tucked them tightly around her, hoping they would keep her warm. I watched her and thought of things that had happened in the months and now years that we'd been in the cellar together.

Miss Abigail was a high-spirited lady from a good family and a good upbringing. She had a good marriage to a good man, a man that Virginia would one day be proud of. She had good respectable children that would marry and have grandchildren that Miss Abigail would have been proud of.

These grandchildren would not know how much their grandmother had begged to be part of her children's lives. Miss Abigail would cry and beg Mr. Ruben and all of us to please let her go back upstairs so she could be with her children. She missed her children and her family very much. It was so sad to see this beautiful child having to live in the cellar. Miss Abigail was not a wild animal that needed to be penned up.

Sometimes I feel that is how some of them felt about her. Mr. Ruben's mother had only been down in the cellar one time, and she wouldn't even come in all the way. She only came down the cellar steps, stared at Miss Abigail, and then quickly left. That was not long after Mr. Ruben put her down here.

Some of them acted like they didn't even care. Well, the Lord cares for Miss Abigail and he will take care of her forever and ever. My sweet Miss Abigail has lost her mind. Don't know what caused her to be so bad off. Don't know why she had such rages. And now she's got so weak that she will never get better. I hope her grandchildren will be as proud of her as they will be of their grandfather, for I know that one day he will be a great man.

I tried to get her to suck on a wet cloth, something wet to her mouth. Her lips had now become dry, cracked, and would bleed. She's such a little thing now. In the last year she has become so confused, and she was so angry and so afraid. And what is so sad is she never knew why she was living in the cellar.

I have cried and cried for her. I think the hardest thing has been not knowing why she was so sick in her mind. I love this child and always have. Miss Abigail don't deserve this. She don't need to be treated like she is nobody, treated like she has no feelings. Miss Abigail had feelings. She had lots of them. But I don't know if everybody wanted to listen to her feelings. She had lots of feelings ever since she was put in the cellar, feelings she never understood.

For a long time Miss Abigail felt like nobody wanted to be around her. She told me many times that she couldn't understand why Mr. Ruben never stayed down here with her for very long. For the first two or three months Mr. Ruben would spend some nights with her, but then that didn't last too long. He always seemed to be going somewhere. I don't know, but for a long time now I don't think Mr. Ruben's thoughts , I don't think have been completely about things going on at Cedar Grove.

Mr. Ruben does have so much on his mind, and I think Dr. Duke wanted to send Miss Abigail to Williamsburg to live in a place, and that was something that Mr. Ruben did not want to do. I don't think it was a very clean place and Mr. Ruben did not like that. I think he wanted Miss Abigail here with us no matter what.

I guess Mr. Ruben did all he knew to do. I remember the day that Dr. Duke told him he thought it would be best for

Miss Abigail to be sent to the new hospital in Williamsburg. Mr. Ruben cried and cried. Mr. Ruben did not know we knew that, but Old Joe had walked up on Mr. Ruben after Dr. Duke had left. Old Joe said he just turned away and went the other way, cause he did not want Mr. Ruben to see him.

Even back then it was like Miss Abigail was not right in her mind. She would get all out of control. None of us could handle her. We tried, but we could not control her by ourselves.

As Miss Abigail lay there I watched her almost lifeless body. She tried one more time to reach out for my hand. I told her I was not going to leave her, and I told her that Mr. Ruben would be there soon.

She didn't even know what I was saying, then she softly and so very slowly spoke the first words that she had spoken in days. She told me she wanted her liberty.

I told her I knew that was what she wanted and I promised her that she would have it soon. I told her she would be free as she once was. Then I felt her thin little fingertips bush against my hand as Miss Abigail got her liberty.

As I held her thin limp little body close to my breast I rocked her and sang softly to her. My sweet Miss Abigail was gone. She was free of the cellar now, free to wander among the woods and the wildflowers as she did so many times before she got sick. Free to be with her children again in a way that she could be happy. And in a way that she could have her freedom.

As I held her close to me, her beautiful black hair hung gently across my arm. I pressed her sweet little face against my cheek and said goodbye to the sweet girl that I had loved and cared for over the last three years.

As she lay in my arms with all of her life drained from her, I felt a sense of happiness—happiness cause she won't have to beg anybody ever again to let her out of the cellar, and she won't have to beg to be able to be with her children again.

As I continued to rock her in my arms Mr. Ruben came busting through the door. He stood there motionless, covered with ice that was dripping from his water-soaked clothes. When he saw her limp little body he fell to his knees and screamed, "No, Abby, no!" All he could do was scream her name and say over and over that he had rode as hard as he could to get back to her.

With tears running down Mr. Ruben's face and his body so weak with grief he could hardly stand, he finally made his way to Miss Abigail. He told me to lay Miss Abigail in his arms. He slowly walked to her bed and laid her down softly. Then he straightened her little cotton shift and ran his fingers through her beautiful long hair as if to comfort her.

With his body trembling he bent down and removed his water-soaked boots. With more tears running down his face he began taking off his wet, icy coat. He then slowly and gently lay down beside Miss Abigail. He put his arm around her and held her close to him. Mr. Ruben then closed his eyes and began to cry again. I turned around and left Miss Abigail's room and closed the door behind me.

I knew by now it had to be close to dawn. I went to wake up Old Joe, but he was already awake. He said he had heard Mr. Ruben ride up. While talking to Old Joe, Sally walked up.

Sally was so upset she had forgotten to cover herself from the weather. Her clothes were quickly covered with sleet and what looked to be a dusting of snow.

While waiting in my room for Mr. Ruben, I heard Miss Abigail's father and mother's wagon pull up. It had taken them longer to get to Cedar Grove. When the wagon was coming in I went outside to greet them. When they saw me they knew their daughter had passed.

Miss Abigail's mother was not that well and was getting up in age. She was so grief stricken that Sally and Chassy had to take her in the house to get warm by the fire and make sure she lay down for a while before seeing her daughter.

When Mr. Ruben did walk out of Miss Abigail's room the only thing he said was, "Will you get Abby ready? I'll get her clothes."

The man looked like death himself. Poor Mr. Ruben was just standing there as if he did not know what to do next. He was a pale gray color, as if the blood had been drained from his veins.

The only way I had ever seen Mr. Ruben was in a strong way. He always knew what to do, but not this time. He stood there and never spoke a word. He stood there looking like a lost boy looking for his mother.

While waiting on Mr. Ruben to leave the cellar, Mr. Madison came running in. The poor boy was screaming. He did not know what to do. The boy was crying so hard for his mother he stumbled down the cellar steps trying to make his way to his father.

When Mr. Madison did reach his father, Mr. Ruben was still standing in the same spot. He had not moved. It was as if he were a piece of stone. I didn't think Mr. Ruben would make it out of the cellar before falling out. Mr. Madison didn't say another word. He just wiped the tears from his face the best he could and took a hold of his father's arm and helped him up the steps out of the cellar.

Chassy and I waited on Benson and another boy to bring a small table down to the cellar. Chassy and I lifted Miss Abigail from her bed and laid her on a piece of clean linen that we had placed across the table. I wanted to get my sweet Miss Abigail ready to leave the cellar forever. As we washed her and brushed her hair Chassy and I both got sick a few times and had to leave the cellar for a few minutes.

It was hard on both of us to do what had to be done. It broke my heart to see her lying there. She was such a good woman, taken out of the life of love she had for everyone and put in a life she never understood. None of us did. Nothing made sense of the life she had to live, taken away from everything she ever knew.

As I was getting her ready I thought back on all the times she would tell me how she could hear the children and their voices coming from upstairs, and the times when she could see them out back through her windows. At one point, I didn't think I was going to be able to do what had to be done.

Her innocent little body was just lying there, but I knew me and Miss Abigail had been through so much that I couldn't leave her now cause she still needed me. I have to say that in one way, although it breaks my heart, I'm glad Miss Abigail had passed. Cause her passing was the only way she could get her freedom. All her pain and all her heartaches are now gone. She had suffered for years in the cellar.

XX
MISS ABIGAIL'S BURIAL

It was a few days before Mr. Ruben buried his Abby. They were waiting on Miss Isabel and other family to get to Cedar Grove. Mr. Ruben was not sure how many more years he would stay at Cedar Grove now that Miss Abigail had passed.

He wanted to bury his Abby in the Lewis cemetery at Evergreen. That's where Mr. Ruben's grandparents and two brothers were already buried, and his parents would be too.

But for some reason Mr. Ruben did not do that. Nobody knows exactly why. He buried Miss Abigail not too far from the cellar. Benson and two other young boys had dug the grave early that morning. As I watched them I couldn't understand why Mr. Ruben wanted to bury her there.

Then Mr. Ruben told Miss Abigail's father that there would be no marker on her grave. I know that hurt Miss Abigail's father when Mr. Ruben told him that. It hurt me too. What was Mr. Ruben thinking? Poor Miss Abigail, in an unmarked grave—how sad that no one would know where she was. That was not right, Mr. Ruben doing that.

I think later on that spring a yellow jasmine was planted over her grave. No one ever said it, but I believe Mr. Madison planted that for his mother. Lord knows that boy sure loved his mother, and I know it broke his heart that there was no marker on her grave.

It was such a sad day for all of us when they carried Miss Abigail out of the cellar. Mr. Ruben didn't even put her upstairs for people to see her. Miss Abigail's mother begged Mr. Ruben to put her daughter in the front parlor so they could sit with her and other family, but Mr. Ruben would not hear of it. He told all of us that Miss Abigail would be kept in the cellar till they put her in the wagon.

When they put Miss Abigail in the wagon Mr. Ruben and the children walked slowly behind. Old Joe and Chassy walked with Miss Abigail's mother and father for fear they might fall. Chassy had to hold on to Miss Abigail's mother's arm cause she was getting weak.

Sally was so upset she did not go to the grave. It was hard on me too, but I had to be there when they put her in the ground. Mr. Ruben got weak again when they were lowering her pine box.

Old Joe had wanted to carve something pretty on the top of Miss Abigail's box, but Mr. Ruben told him there was no need for that. Old Joe said that brought tears to his eyes when Mr. Ruben told him that. Said it shocked him to hear those words.

Mr. Madison was holding his father's arm for fear Mr. Ruben would pass out from grief. Mr. Madison was a man himself, so he knew what love his father and mother shared. Poor Mr. Ruben, I didn't think he would hold up.

After they buried Miss Abigail we didn't see Mr. Ruben for days—many days. He kept to his room. Sally would take his food to him and hoped he would eat. Sometimes he would and sometimes he would not. So much grief was still inside of him. I think he loved Miss Abigail with everything he had.

As the months went on Mr. Ruben stayed as busy as he could. He didn't talk much about Miss Abigail. I think it was cause of the kind of sickness that she had, and the things he had to do to keep things under control. I think all of that was on his mind. They were things he didn't want to do, but had to do. I know he thought of these things many times.

He asked me months later after Miss Abigail's passing, did I think he made the right choice by not sending his Abby to that place in Williamsburg. I told him that I thought he did the right thing by keeping Miss Abigail at Cedar Grove.

Those three years that Miss Abigail had to live in the cellar, her death, and all the months that followed were so painful for all of us. No one knows how it was. We are all close here at Cedar Grove, so we all did whatever we needed to do.

XXI
EDMUND'S WALK

Little Edmund is growing up. He is eight years old now and still has beautiful eyes like his mother—those dark black eyes. His hair has gotten darker than it was five years ago at the time of Miss Abigail's death. His little face reminds me so much of his mother—such a sweet face. Edmund is so loving and caring, just like Miss Abigail was.

He is growing tall like his father and his older brother Madison. He will be a handsome young man. Miss Abigail would be so proud of him. He studies a lot and likes to read as much as she did.

In the last five years Mr. Madison and Miss Jane have married. They have two daughters, Miss Elizabeth Anne, after Jane's grandmother, and Miss Abigail Louise, after Miss Abigail and Catherine Louise. They are pretty children. I hope I live long enough to tell those children about their Grandmother Lewis.

Miss Martha Elizabeth and Miss Catherine Louise are both married now. Miss Martha Elizabeth married Thomas Hughes and lives close to Charlottesville. She doesn't get to visit us much as she would like, but when she does we sit and talk about her mother. Miss Abigail's death and the years leading up to her death were very, very hard on those young girls.

Miss Catherine Louise lives closer over in Goochland County, so she gets to visit more. Her husband, Benjamin Payne, was left his grandfather's plantation, so that's where they're living. Catherine Louise said it backs up to the river. I'm sure it's a nice place.

I don't know if Miss Sarah will marry or not, but she is still young. I don't think she has menfolks on her mind right yet. She really likes her studies and her music. She likes her music like Miss Abigail and Mr. Ruben did, and both of them were very good at it. We could be out in the yard close to the main house and we could hear the music.

Miss Judith Anne's family is growing more each year. All the Bacons have large families. She is still a pretty woman. Her and some of her children stayed here at Cedar Grove with us for quite a while after Miss Abigail's death. She wanted to do whatever she could do to help with her younger sisters and brother. She was always a loving child too.

Miss Sally has passed in the last five years. I think the way Miss Abigail had to live the last three years of her life was just too much for Sally. Sally was getting older and her pain about Miss Abigail was too hard on her. Sally always thought of Miss Abigail as the young girl she helped raise at Mount Laurel. When us women slaves would get together, Sally would always talk about when Miss Abigail was a young girl. Sally also had a rough life at Sweet Pine before going to Mount Laurel, so I know that added years to Sally.

Mr. Ruben seems to be gone most of the time now. He

enjoys his talks with people and still talks as much as ever. Everybody talks about him and says that Ruben Lewis is a smart man. I think most people like Mr. Ruben. I think I know more about what he does now. He is so busy, but he seems to like it.

I was so surprised when Mr. Ruben told me and the other slaves that we would be leaving Cedar Grove soon. Mr. Ruben has bought another plantation closer to Williamsburg. He said that would give him more time to be with Sarah and Edmund. He said it would make his traveling quicker.

I cried the day he told us we would be leaving soon. I asked Edmund if he would like to walk down the path his mother used to take before she got sick. I wanted to talk to him about his mother; Edmund never knew anything about his mother. He doesn't even remember her. He was three years old when Miss Abigail died. I know Mr. Ruben has told him a few things, but I wanted to share some other things about his mother with him.

As me and little Edmund walked down the path I began telling him how much his mother loved him, and how sorry she was that she could not come upstairs and live with him. I told him Miss Abigail got sick in the mind and that's why she couldn't stay with him

I also told him that his father did everything he could do to help his mother, but no matter what he did it did not help.

As we walked among the cedar trees I told him his father had named their plantation Cedar Grove because of all the cedar trees that were growing all around. He asked me did his mother like the smell of cedar. I told him yes, she sure did. I told little Edmund a story of how Miss Abigail liked it when the boys would bring lots of cedar for her fire. He said yes, he liked it too.

As we walked we reached a small clearing in the woods where Miss Abigail, Uncle Pete, and me would stop sometime. It was a place where Uncle Pete would pick some wildflowers for Miss Abigail. I told him how Uncle Pete would sometimes bring his mother wildflowers and she would put them in her window so the sunlight would shine on them.

Miss Abigail would say, "The sunlight makes them have more color." She would look at them while staring out her windows. She would watch what was going on out back. She would watch the running of the plantation or sometimes just watch the children playing.

As we walked little Edmund's eyes began to water. I knew he missed his mother, even if he didn't know her. I took his little hand and held it in mine. It was as if I was holding Miss Abigail's hand. It felt like her thin little hand the night she got her liberty.

I told him not to be sad, but try to think of happy things that would have happened with him and his mother if she had not got sick. I told him that she had tried real hard to hold on to life so she could get well. But she didn't have the strength in her body or in her mind to do that. Her body and her mind had become so weak. She wanted help, but there was no help that could come.

I kept holding his little hand as we walked deeper into the woods. I told him his mother was free now, free to wander among the woods like she did before she had to live in the cellar.

I told little Edmund that when he becomes a man and has a family to make sure he tells his children all about his mother Abigail. I told him to make sure and tell them she was a beautiful lady who loved Edmund very much. One day, maybe he and his children could take one more walk down the path in the woods that Miss Abigail loved so much.

CPSIA information can be obtained
at www.ICGtesting.com
Printed in the USA
BVHW081320130620
581307BV00004B/175